Ancient Ties

Book 2, Pale Moonlight

By Marie Johnston

GW00778203

Ancient Ties

Born to be Guardians...

Chayton Eagle comes from a strong line of wolf shifters, his father an ancient in their pack. Chayton proudly acts as a Guardian, defending the colonies from danger—both from outsiders and from threats inside the pack. The one thing he doesn't need is a human-raised female on his team—especially not one who passes out each time she shifts! Never mind that she was trained by elite Guardians, Chayton doesn't need the distraction of a tall, sexy-as-hell redhead when he's working. He has to focus. And he has to remember he's scheduled to take the blood oath with a female, a long-ago pairing arranged by her parents. It doesn't matter he and Kaitlyn are fated mates.

She can't be his. Not now. Not ever.

Destined to be Mates.

Kaitlyn Savoy knows Chayton is supposed to be her mate. Too bad he's such an ass about her human upbringing making her weak. Too bad she's been assigned as his partner to take down the feral shifters threatening one of the colonies. Too bad she's so damn attracted to him. As the mission continues, Chayton is captured by the ferals, and Kaitlyn proves her worth as a Guardian. During the rescue, she uncovers the secrets of her past, secrets that will affect her future. Despite his best efforts, Chayton's opinion of her begins to change, his respect growing—along with feelings he can't deny. She's become part of his life, part of his heart. A fact his soon-to-be inlaws notice—and they intend

to put an end to the temptation Kaitlyn poses to Chayton.
No matter what.

For new release updates, chapter sneak peeks, and exclusive quarterly short stories, sign up for Marie's newsletter at www.mariejohnstonwriter.com and receive download links for the book that started it all, Fever Claim, and three short stories of characters from the series.

To my critique group, Wet Ink. Always there for laughs, questions, and support even though you're across the country.

Chapter One

"Aww, fuck. *You're* cooking?"

Kaitlyn Savoy cringed at the male's voice. So unfair that Chayton Eagle's deep rumble and unique cadence made her nerve endings tingle, while his cocky swagger propelled her anger off the charts.

"You're welcome," she shot back, sugar dripping from her tone. "I'm sure the others will appreciate not having to dig fish bones out of their food like when it's your night to cook."

Chayton propped his hip on the counter. She didn't have to look at him to know his glimmering sorrel eyes swept her body, as good as a feather whispering over her skin.

She ignored him while waiting for her quinoa to boil. Negative feelings about her cooking weren't restricted to Chayton; the others didn't appreciate anything that didn't have a face before it died. Once the water boiled, she set the lid on top.

With a fortifying breath, she faced the tall male. The planes and angles of his face were every bit the Native American warriors he descended from. The long braid trailing down his back didn't detract from his masculinity, but enhanced it, in her opinion, which had no business offering insight into his looks.

She flipped her own braided hair over her shoulder and crossed her arms. "No matter what the guys around here say, grains and vegetables are good for shifters, too. Just because you've all devoured meat with a side of meat for decades doesn't mean it's healthy for you."

His upper lip rose in a sneer. "Spoken like a human."

Oh, the guy crawled under skin and pricked at her! "Yeah, it is. But I'm still a shifter, regardless of being raised human."

He plucked a piece of bacon off the platter she'd set aside to drain. She lunged to swat his hand, but he popped it into his mouth and chewed with a shit-eating grin.

Add another offense to his growing list. The bacon was to be chopped into the quinoa to coerce the baconphiles she lived with to broaden their food horizon. She'd cooked five pounds and no matter how much Chayton extolled the benefits of fish, he'd eat half in minutes. He'd done it to her before.

She slid the plate away from him.

He flashed another grin that bared a hint of fang. Her stomach flipped. She ignored that, too. Just like she always dismissed her body's reactions around Chayton.

"Uh, you were raised human *and* you act human." His gaze taunted her.

Ah, yes. His favorite hobby of pointing out her humanity. He treated it like a stain on her soul. She rolled her eyes to show him he didn't get to her, when in fact she was developing a nice inferiority complex—but only around him.

"You're in my way, Eagle." She waited for him to move, knowing he'd make that a fight, too.

He cocked an eyebrow. "What? We get more than nuts and berries tonight?"

His Native American accent grew more pronounced whenever he was picking on her. Her secret shame was that she almost looked forward to her confrontations with him so she could hear it, and not because it meant he was irritated.

The way his voice deepened and stressed each syllable with a little kick… It'd be more enchanting if he wasn't usually insulting her when it happened.

Their little game of chicken where no one moved ended when he finally pushed away from the drawer so she could find the tongs she needed for the steaks. The meat, which was coming to room temperature on the table, was in plain sight, so he knew full well *nuts and berries* weren't on the menu.

He might've moved out of her way, but he hadn't left the kitchen. While it was a large area meant to cook for several people, it shrank to a quarter of its size with his presence.

She flipped steaks onto the grill one at a time, savoring the sizzle with each landing. "Why are you still here?"

"Why aren't you grilling outside; it's beautiful out. In my culture, we're outside every chance we get."

Again with the culture stuff. "Maybe you should go fishing, Eagle, prep for your assigned night to cook."

His gaze sharpened on her like it did every time she used his last name. He placed one hand on the countertop next to her and his other hand on his hip, drawing her attention to his muscular, yet lanky, frame. He would never out-bulk any of the other male Guardians in the pack, but his body still rippled with lean muscles.

She ripped her gaze off him before he thought she was actually interested in him and rewarded her with his disdain.

"I have been *hokuwa*—that's fishing. I've had to start freezing my catches." His mouth twisted as if the thought disgusted him. "But everyone here eats more than I catch in a week."

Even with so many new additions to their pack, they each still ended up cooking almost weekly. Most were mated and couples got to share cooking duties versus splitting two nights. Kaitlyn didn't mind. She loved her job as a Guardian—a shifter cop for the surrounding packs. But cooking duty meant no one was trying to fight her.

Well, except for Chayton, but it wasn't physical. Grappling with him would be…

Thankfully, he spoke before that thought train took off. "The guys complain about scales and fins, but they eat fish by the ton."

She flipped the steaks. A sear on each side and raw in the middle was how everyone liked them. She preferred a little less bleeding in her food, but according to Chayton, that was the human part of her talking.

"You could, you know, *buy* the fish," she pointed out.

He made a disgusted noise and his face reflected it tenfold. "To catch and gather what we eat is a significant aspect of our nature. Not buying a hunk of stockyard raised cattle sitting on a slab of Styrofoam and covered in cellophane. I kill what I cook." He bared another fang and her butterflies took off. "If I even cook it at all."

Yuck. The backlash of not knowing she was a shifter until her early twenties: she couldn't stand raw meat. And that was exactly why he said it.

"Then run off and fetch supper instead of bitching about mine."

"I will, but the commander called and wanted me to wait here until he could talk to both of us."

She flattened her lips. It hadn't escaped her notice that Chayton rarely ate with them. Some of their crew often ate in their own cabin, whether personal preference or it was just easier and more intimate with loved ones. But Chayton dined in on

~10~

his night only. Was it a sign he rejected them and being a part of their pack, or because he was a control freak with his food?

Commander Fitzsimmons entered the kitchen. "Chayton, Kaitlyn, I need a minute."

"Sure, boss." Kaitlyn gave him her full attention, difficult with Chayton around, as she finished prepping dinner.

Chayton tracked her every move. "Commander."

Fitzsimmons was the one male in the pack whom Chayton never used a less than reverent tone with: not only was the commander the boss, but he was one of the oldest in their pack. He rarely cracked a smile—okay, she'd never seen him smile—and his ruddy complexion amplified his stolid demeanor.

"A colony northwest of us has been having problems with a group of rogue shifters who are deteriorating into becoming feral. The colony leader thought they could handle them, but last night they lost ten people, three of them pack leaders and one clan leader. The majority were females and children." The commander's grim hazel gaze pinned them both. "I need you two on it."

Kaitlyn's mind whirred. "They targeted females and young? Is anyone missing?"

Commander Fitzsimmons's eyes lit with approval at her deduction. "Yes. Two females. The colony fought 'em off, but the leaders suspect, as do I, that they'll be hit again. It's a forested region, a perfect place for our kind, so it's scattered with colonies."

Chayton had gone unusually still, his gaze piercing the commander, but not seeing him. "When do you want us to go?"

Us. She had to go on a distance mission with Chayton Eagle. Twenty-four/seven exposure to what she went through the last fifteen minutes.

Her boss's gaze flicked to Chayton. "It's not your colony, but it's not far away. I'm concerned they'll become a target."

Chayton's tone sharpened to a deadly edge. "I dare them to hit my colony."

"You need to stop them before that happens. It's a four-hour drive. Take off after you eat. I want you in the vicinity in case they're attacked again. Talk to them. Take a look around, then get those females back."

Kaitlyn nodded and flipped the second batch of steaks. She peeked up at Chayton, who stood motionless. His bronzed skin had developed an ashen tint.

The commander's intense gaze captured them both. "This won't be a problem."

He wasn't asking. It was a warning that vibrated through his voice.

"I'm a professional, Commander," she said, concentrating on cooking. It wouldn't help getting upset if she looked at Chayton's reaction.

Out of the corner of her eye, her nemesis inclined his head. An ambiguous way to say yes, it was a problem, but he'd deal?

"Good," the commander replied. "Report when you arrive."

"You got it, boss." Kaitlyn would not let Chayton ruin this job or her position in the pack. The males she worked with were her family, their mates her closest friends. They were all she had in this world, and she owed them more than they ever knew.

Chayton hissed under his breath. "I gotta go deep in the forest where we're going to hunt wild shifters with the girl who passes out after each shift."

She clenched her jaw. There it was. Her secret shame and the other major reason he couldn't stand her.

"I'll go pack," he snarled. "Meet me in twenty."

She willed herself not to tell him to stuff himself with his inflated ego until he choked. She'd been a Guardian for less than three years; he had seniority. She had to at least pretend to get along with him.

He stalked out of the kitchen. Kaitlyn released her breath. Gut through this mission. It'd be over soon enough.

Chayton stormed to his cabin.

A four-hour drive. With Kaitlyn.

Spending the night. With Kaitlyn.

Roaming the woods. With Kaitlyn.

His heart pounded, his nostrils flared, and he huffed like a bear after a marathon. Slamming his front door open, he charged through and kicked it shut behind him.

Only then did he double over, hands on his knees, sagging to catch his breath.

Kaitlyn Savoy.

The sexiest thing he'd ever laid eyes on.

The shifter he was never supposed to meet. His mate.

And she was oblivious to it.

He stomped through his cabin. Her lack of mating insight was for the best. If he had his pick of shifters, she'd be the last on the list. Besides, he was promised to another. Kaitlyn was young yet, and based on her blasé-to-distasteful reaction to him, she'd have no trouble moving on. Or not. Her sanity may last longer than most who don't anchor their souls with a mate. But if she needed to bond, she wouldn't have a problem finding someone. Like that bartender at Pale Moonlight.

His fangs bared and a growl escaped before he stopped himself. Chayton had never caught her with him, but stories had it the bartender helped her assuage the physical needs experienced by shifters of their caliber. She hadn't been with the guy in the months Chayton had been around. That decision had increased the bartender's life expectancy considerably.

No. *No.* It shouldn't matter. She would find someone to mate with and he had no say with whom. Chayton straightened and wiped his brow dotted with sweat. It was always an effort to contain his reaction around that female.

Why her?

Ancient blood—pure, undiluted shifter blood—ran through his veins, thanks to his father. His Sioux mother would roll over in her grave. Chayton's bloodlines were rich with history and honor.

The female he'd sworn himself to, Tika, would make a lovely mate instead. Soft brown eyes, feminine curves, and ancestry as strong as his. In fact, she was coming of age soon. For him, that was twenty-five. Her parents had pushed for their union when she turned eighteen, but that had seemed too pervy for him. At two hundred twenty-nine, he wasn't about to jump a girl the second she was legal. If it was up to him, he'd wait even longer, but even Tika had pushed for their binding.

His stomach rumbled, alerting him that he'd missed dinner. Not that he'd eat at the main lodge anyway; it was a tactic he used to avoid Kaitlyn.

He trudged to his fridge and pulled out two plates of walleye. He'd caught them early this morning, his favorite time to fish. After tossing a skillet on the stove to heat up, he went in search of his overnight bag. Not much was really needed. He was a low maintenance guy.

His lip curled. Kaitlyn would probably have a suitcase that weighed fifty pounds. She was a notorious shopper and he'd heard her cabin was bursting at the log seams. Packing done, he drifted into the kitchen and tossed his fish on to fry. While the fish cooked, he took out the elastic band at the bottom of his hair, unraveled the braid, finger-combed it, and then parted it down the middle. Separately, he braided each side into the traditional two of his mother's people.

His people. He'd keep his promise to his mom. Carry on their ways. It had hurt her enough when he'd had to leave for Guardian training, a job that kept him away from home. The least he could do was carry on their bloodline.

Once his hair was done, he flipped his fish out of the pan onto a plate. He leaned against his kitchen counter to eat. Most of the West Creek Guardians thought his eating habits were primitive, probably assumed he ate everything raw. And, yeah, sometimes. But his mother raised him to be civil, too.

After he finished eating and cleaned his dishes, he glanced around his cabin, making sure nothing else needed to be done before he left. His cabin echoed his heritage, and that he was a bachelor. Sparse decorations were scattered around the main area, while partially completed beadwork and feather art scattered the surfaces. Mostly, he preferred leather-working, like the satchel he'd packed his gear in.

He hefted his bag and steeled himself for flashing green eyes and full lips that held back a lot of Kaitlyn's comments. Oh, he'd see them, churning in her eyes, but her sense of duty prevented her from spilling them.

A trait he tried not to admire her for.

Trotting to the lodge, he aimed for the garage stall where he could pick up his SUV. When he pulled out of the garage, Kaitlyn was waiting, one hand shoved in a pants pocket, backpack slung over her shoulder, rifle bag in her hand. He looked around, but she had no other luggage.

She tossed her gear in the back and hopped in, bringing her honeysuckle scent with her. The cloying fragrance wrapped around him, tightening his gut. His fists clenched around the wheel. He hated flowers. He hated flowers. He hated flowers.

"Who ate your Wheaties?" Her gaze roamed his face and ran down the length of his braids. His scalp prickled, like she'd given them a hard tug…as if he were on top of her—

Sweet Mother, no. He'd sworn no more of those fantasies. From experience, there wasn't a lake big enough to douse that arousal.

He glared at her to mask the desire he felt. "I don't eat cereal. I had fish."

Her nose wrinkled. "I can tell."

A scowl creased his brow. He stomped down on the gas and sped off. A smirk twisted her lips. He narrowed his eyes on her, but couldn't stop from tilting his head slightly to sniff at himself.

She relaxed in the seat and pulled out her phone. "Do you know where we're going? I think the commander texted the location."

"Yep." Chayton stared out the window, hoping she'd drop it at that.

"Oh yeah. You're from that area, right?"

He made a noncommittal grunt and avoided looking at her. That damn shirt she wore, with the gun holsters strapped around her breasts like a frame, showed off her best asset. It would be better if the Tomb Raider sat next to him. At least he could fuck her, leave satisfied, and not dwell on it again.

The redhead next to him... Her long braid reached below her shoulders, hitting the same point on her back that his braids hit on him.

She'd never once made a crack about his hair. No one did, actually. It was like they all saw the color of his skin, his swarthy features, and solemn expression, and left him the fuck alone. Just the way he liked.

They drove in silence. At this time of night, there was little traffic in West Creek. He steered across the bridge in Freemont and turned onto the highway that would take them to the headwaters of the river that separated the two cities. From there, they'd head deeper into the forest where many shifter colonies made their home.

Several miles out of town, Kaitlyn poked on the radio station. Country music blared. Old school country, when fringe was as long as the sideburns.

Chayton's favorite.

"Ooh, I love this stuff." The smile in her voice warmed his insides.

He pushed the scan button to turn the station.

"Hey." She glowered at him, then rolled her eyes. "Of course you don't like it."

"Why would I?" Other than for the steady beat and smooth, deep voices of the country crooners, or the sassy lyrics. More importantly... "Why would you like it?"

She crossed her arms and stared out her window at passing trees, which were growing thicker with each mile.

"So? Why?" He didn't know why he prodded, other than the burning drive to find out why she enjoyed the same thing he did. "You weren't even born close to when this music played."

A muscle in her jaw tensed. Her reluctance at spilling her reasons drove his curiosity higher.

"Come on, Kaitlyn. All I'm asking is why you like classic country."

She shifted her eyes to him. What startled him was the deep-rooted sadness he saw there.

"My mom used to listen to it. She'd laugh and dance around. We'd two-step around the living room." A hesitant smile lifted her mouth, but faded away. "It reminds me of the good times, before my dad took it all away."

His brows shot up in shock. It wasn't like Kaitlyn to share her personal history. None of the other Guardians had shared it, either. Chayton assumed they either didn't know, or it didn't matter, that a pretty girl like her grew up without a care in the world.

"Did you end up kicking his ass after you got your first black belt?" Mark down the first time he tried to lighten the mood around her, or for her.

"Didn't have a chance. He killed my mom and himself when I was eleven."

Chayton barked out a "Holy shit." He cleared his throat, feeling like an ass for turning the station. "What the hell for?"

She shrugged with no effort behind the movement. "Dunno."

A small sigh escaped him. He punched in the station to return it to the classic country channel.

She glanced at the radio, and then at him. Her surprise filled the cab.

His considerate gesture was a shock to him, too. This mission couldn't end soon enough. And Sweet Mother Earth, they'd better not have to go to his colony. The last thing he needed was Kaitlyn exposed to his pack.

Chapter Two

Searing lips burned a path down her neck. Kaitlyn smiled, murmuring for him to continue. A rock-hard body descended upon her. So close. She'd been wanting him inside of her forever. She'd felt empty for so long, nothing and no one had been able to fill the void, until she met him.

"Kaitlyn." His voice. So familiar.

"More."

His head lifted and she gazed into dark brown eyes. The slide of his braids caressed her chest.

Braids?

Her eyes popped open with a gasp. She was in a vehicle and Chayton was driving, and she'd fallen asleep.

He shot her a questioning look out of the corner of his eye. "I thought your snoring was bad enough, but you scare the shit out of me when you wake up like that, Cinnamon."

"Cinnamon?" She wiped her mouth to make sure she hadn't drooled while she napped. The wet dream about her partner was bad enough.

Why did her regular partner have to be tied up with family issues? She thought of Jace Stockwell like a brother. They worked well together and Jace accepted all of her quirks. To top it off, his mate was her best friend. Instead she was stuck with Mr. Personality, a shifter her body refused to listen to her mind about.

"You call me Eagle. I thought I should come up with something."

Night had fallen while she slept. She tried not to stare at his stark profile, cast in shadows. Strong nose, high cheekbones, perpetual scowl.

He took his eyes off the road to cock an eyebrow at her.

Oh, she'd been staring. She wrestled her gaze back to the road. "Eagle's your last name."

"But calling you Savoy isn't as fun." His gaze swept her body, then his forehead creased like he couldn't believe he'd just done that. "Cinnamon fits your hair."

Whoa. That was *maybe* a compliment. Warmth crept up her spine. She struggled to change the subject. "How close are we to the colony?"

"Valley Moon is twenty miles away, but we're turning off the highway in a couple of miles. The roads are probably still poorly maintained and narrow."

She regarded his stiff posture. "Are you worried about your home?"

Chayton snorted with derision. "The rogues can try to attack my colony and they *will* regret it."

"I hope so," she muttered. Out the window, cottonwoods had long changed to evergreens. Not

~22~

the countryside she was used to. Spread out under moonlight, the forest's beauty glowed. "Since we're up here, we can stop in for a welfare check."

"I'm *not* bringing you to the colony." Venom laced his voice.

Kaitlyn stared at him, her insecurity cracked a little wider. "What is your problem with me?"

He maneuvered a turn and sped along a bumpy road that looked gobbled up by trees. A muscle ticked in his jaw. She waited.

"Bloodlines are…important…in my pack *and* in my clan. In all the packs that comprise my clan. All the clans that make up my colony, really."

"So? I'm a natural-born Guardian. I'd say that's bloodline enough."

One muscled shoulder lifted in a half-hearted shrug. "Not really. My dad's an ancient. He met my mom centuries ago, so her Sioux blood was as pure as it could get. Having to leave the colony because I was destined to be a Guardian wasn't looked upon fondly by my parents, or our leaders."

"Like, a real ancient?" Maybe she was a little impressed. Ancients were more like the werewolves she'd grown up hearing stories of; they were the original wolf-shifter.

"Legit."

"How'd he survive the extinction?"

Chayton's characteristic sneer returned. "Nobody gets to the colony. Not Sigma when they were at their strongest, not the Vampire Council before they lost their backbone, no one."

"I didn't think there were any left, that they got wiped out defending the species against the massive, targeted slaughter."

His nostrils flared and his eyes blazed. His foot crashed down onto the brake and they fishtailed to a stop.

"Holy shit, Eagle." Kaitlyn threw her hands up to brace herself on the dash, grateful that her longevity didn't stop her from using a seatbelt. "What are you doing?"

He turned in his seat to face her, his body vibrating with fury. "Are you saying my father didn't try to defend our people?"

Instead of being intimidated by the livid shifter confronting her, she rolled her eyes. "The shitty way you interpreted an innocent question is not my problem." With each word, she leaned closer to him until inches separated their faces.

This close, his evergreen scent assaulted her. No, not quite evergreen. Like a recently felled tree—freshly cut pine. She lingered through a long inhale, his smell curling into her belly.

His pupils dilated, his anger level dropped when his gaze lowered to her lips. Her breathing stalled. Was he—was he going to kiss her?

A flash of white outside the window ripped her attention away, her Guardian instincts on alert. "What was that?"

Chayton blinked like he was emerging from a fog. In an instant, he shot straight, his expression serious. He pivoted in his seat to follow her gaze.

Kaitlyn opened her door and hopped out. She withdrew her Beretta Compact. Its sleek lines glinted silver in the moonlight.

Chayton emerged from the SUV spitting a stream of cuss words.

Good to know how he felt about getting close to her. At least she had her work. "It looked like a person streaking through the trees."

He hung back. "Seriously, Cinnamon. We're in the middle of shifter country and you think seeing a streaker in the trees is relevant. It's a daily event. I'd be worried if we didn't see anyone running around the woods."

She lowered her gun and thought a moment. "Do you run like a naked human in the middle of the forest? Because what I saw looked humanoid."

Her drive to find out what the flash of flesh was couldn't be ignored. She had to find it. Had to know.

"Fine. You and your guns go hunting in the trees." The derision in his voice rankled her. "I'll shift and do some real hunting."

She bit down on her tongue to keep from telling him to go fuck himself. Her ability to shift was just fine, but her inability to not pass out when she shifted back comprised the foundation of all her insecurities.

The sound of Chayton shedding his clothing had her deliberately turning her back to him. In the months he'd been assigned to their Guardian pack, she hadn't glimpsed him out for his runs. The other shifters she lived with didn't flaunt their assets, but it wasn't uncommon to see a full moon that wasn't in the sky. Not that she'd been scanning the woods around her cabin to catch a glimpse of Chayton in transition.

Narrowing her gaze through the trees, she stalked steadily in the direction the mystery animal had moved. A huge, brown wolf surged past her, disappearing into the darkness. She screwed her mouth up at irony that the color of Chayton's coat resembled a spice.

Cinnamon.

For a second in the vehicle, she could almost believe they were fated mates.

Oh, she *knew*. He didn't think she did, but she'd been around men her whole life and how she felt around him was worlds different. Mated members of her pack always said you just know and it was true.

Before she learned she was a shifter, her innate nature exhibited itself in her rather promiscuous relations with men. Afterward…well, Guardians possessed a stronger sex drive than standard shifters and she was no different. Only, living with shifters made it seem normal because it was.

Snuffling and panting reached her ears as she neared the initial spot she saw the movement.

I smell shifter. Chayton's rich voice floated through her mind like a caress.

Good golly, that was just unfair. She refused to acknowledge their status as mates until he quit being an ass to her. And apologized for his derogatory treatment of her.

But it was hard when he fired up her hormones and steeped them in desire just by mentally speaking a simple phrase.

Just one? She scanned the trees, letting her senses flare out. They weren't as strong as a wolf's, but this way, she wouldn't have to endure Chayton loading her naked ass back into the SUV when they were done searching.

So, you can at least communicate like this? I wasn't sure.

You could've asked.

A mental grunt answered her. *Yes. Just one, male, but he smells different. I can't pinpoint it, like it's familiar on a few different levels, like I've come across this shifter before, but completely foreign.*

Feral? Kaitlyn brushed through some pine branches. They scraped her face and the needles caught on her shirt, but she pushed forward. Crisp air, bordering on cold, dulled the pain to an annoyance. Crouching low, she moved through the trees. If Chayton wasn't so intent on following the trail, he'd likely comment that if she shifted, she wouldn't have to crouch.

She followed him. He trotted, stopping only to sniff and readjust as needed; otherwise, he'd leave her in the dust. Probably on purpose.

The hair on the back of her neck stood up and she slowed. Looking all around her, she couldn't figure out why she was on alert. It wasn't like she sensed danger. Her intuition didn't scream at her to get back to their vehicle, but she had to find out who this shifter was. She swung around and ducked through the branches.

Savoy? Where are you going?

She ignored him and picked up her speed to a run.

The smell of strange shifter grew stronger. A blur of ivory ran off as she neared the edge of the road. "Hey! Stop!"

She prepared to give chase, but the speed of the blur flying through the trees was faster than she'd ever witnessed. Chayton charged past Kaitlyn, startling her. She hadn't realized he'd stopped his search to follow her.

A heartbeat of indecision stalled her. Should she go after him? The strange shifter was faster and Kaitlyn's gut told her he wouldn't catch up to him. That speed was unnatural, even for a paranormal.

Chayton's return saved her from the decision. His flanks heaved with effort, but she also sensed frustration. He flowed into his human form, leaving her slack-jawed at the sight.

He glared into the forest. "He was gone before I even got a read on his trail. I've never seen that before. I bet I could follow him for days and never catch up."

Her mouth snapped shut before he glanced at her. Lean muscle roped his body from head to toe, like a work of art. As he spun to stomp toward his clothing, muscles flexed between his ribs, framing washboard abs. His quads bunched and relaxed when he bent to step into his pants.

"This kind of nudity shouldn't bother shifters." His lilting accent grew thicker with each word.

He'd caught her perusing his body like a night at the museum, after all. Speech escaped her until he straightened to fasten his pants and roll his shirt on.

"How'd you get all those scars?" White puckered marks dotted his chest. Bullet holes. "I thought only silver scarred us."

A brow arched, an arrogant tilt lifted the corner of his mouth. "We call scars *naze*. I'm almost two hundred and thirty. I've been through some shit, seen some wars."

"You're that old?" She strained to see every last inch of his smooth skin before his shirt draped over him. "I mean, you come off as young and cocky. Not even Bennett and Mercury are that old."

Something she said caused him to tense. His right eye twitched. Didn't he like the *young and cocky* statement?

"And you would know Bennett and Mercury intimately?"

She sucked in a breath. How dare he? She'd done nothing wrong, not now, not then. Dealing with him tested all of her patience.

"Hardly. Before I found out about this other world with shifters and vampires and demons, I sought physical relief at Pale Moonlight, just like those two had. I barely remember it. I doubt they do, either. After they met their mates, anyone before them faded away." She didn't need to justify her activities from years ago. Or even last month. So why'd she keep talking? "I owe them everything. They saved my life, trained me, and made me a part of their pack. Their mates are like my sisters and they're like brother-in-laws I respect the hell out of. Who told you?"

Old news was an understatement. In their world, it shouldn't be a big deal. Except to Chayton.

His lip curled in a sneer. He didn't look at her as he buckled on his weapon belt and shoved his feet into his boots. "You're quite the legend at the club. At least with that bartender."

Yeah, Waylon. He'd dropped hints about being exclusive and she'd considered it. It was nice turning to a familiar face when the urges got too strong to ignore. Then Chayton Eagle had been assigned to their pack. Her urges shot through the roof, but she needed to work out her feelings and get over Chayton before she stripped down with anyone else.

Two could go down this line of questioning. "Should we head to your colony so I can find out who you've fucked and confront you about it?"

His eyes flared in alarm, but he recovered quickly.

"No," she continued before he could say anything, "I wouldn't do that. Because it doesn't matter and it's none of my business."

He shot her a glare before opening the SUV door to climb inside, muttering something she thought was, "You'd be surprised about that."

Kaitlyn took her time walking around to the passenger side. This mission couldn't be over soon enough.

***

Chayton eased his grip on the wheel until his knuckles were no longer white. Kaitlyn hadn't said a thing since she'd gotten in. He didn't blame her.

Why'd he go there? Bringing up the two senior males in their Guardian pack was a low blow. To her and them. He thought highly of the entire West Creek Guardian pack—except Kaitlyn, and that was because he couldn't.

From what Chayton had seen, Bennett and Mercury never treated Kaitlyn as anything other than a colleague. She was right, he doubted either of them remembered their single days. Hearts damn near danced in their eyes when they thought of their females.

They crested a hill. In the valley, the lights of the colony stretched in front of them. He breathed a sigh of relief. Some distance from the female next to him couldn't happen fast enough.

He idled into town. Kaitlyn twisted in her seat to look around them. Valley Moon was a quaint colony, equipped with some modern updates, but evidence of the ravage lay scattered through the streets.

A once-sizable building to their left that had probably been a store littered the sidewalk and road. Wood and brick tumbled over the pavement like its foundation was ripped out from underneath, then lit on fire. Small fires still burned on both sides of the street, their trails of smoke wisping into the night sky.

Several shifters paused in their clean up efforts to glance at them, but must've sensed they were Guardians.

She scanned the street, eyes wide. "How many rogue shifters can do this much damage?"

Chayton maneuvered the SUV around the blackened, charred remnants and whistled low. "Either a few pissed off rogues or just some crazed ferals. It'd only take one to cause the vandalism while one or two went on a killing rampage."

"Or they snuck in and started the fires to use them as a distraction to murder at will."

It was the likely scenario and he grudgingly respected her assumption.

Another building to their right still smoldered under the stars. The beaten-down sign read only one legible word: *healing*.

Chayton pursed his lips and shook his head. The healer's building being demolished wasn't a coincidence.

Kaitlyn's grim expression mirrored his own. "Whoever did this targeted the mainstays of the town. Shifters might not need doctors, but we still rely on them to expedite healing. Our own Doc stays plenty busy with our pack. But Valley Moon won't have anywhere to get aid or—" she gestured over her shoulder at the felled building they'd just passed, "—obtain fresh food and supplies."

"One of the things we need to find out is whether they targeted the females and young to kill or to kidnap."

"Two females were taken."

"I know," he said, his tone grim. "We'll find them, if they haven't yet."

"I didn't smell other shifters on that animal we encountered."

"Nope. He's a separate problem. Maybe the colony knows something about him."

Chayton arrived at the address the commander had given them. A tall, burly shifter limped out. Chayton swore under his breath as he and Kaitlyn got out. The male's pale features divulged the pain he was in from the ravaged leg he supported himself on. He'd had a full day to heal, yet his body still had a lot of mending to do.

"Guardians," the male's voice resonated. From the powerful aura surrounding him, he was the colony leader. "Come inside."

He pivoted gingerly to head back inside, expecting them to follow.

Chayton glanced at Kaitlyn. Her scrutiny left the small building to sweep their surroundings. As much as Chayton wanted to hold her shifter inadequacies against her, she was an excellent Guardian. Not that he'd ever tell her.

His senses flared out. Chaos lingered on the heavy air hanging over the colony. Breathing in through his mouth, he tasted death and sadness, but a current of pride carried through. Typical for most colonies. If pride was missing, or wasn't the base emotion he sensed, it usually meant trouble in one way or another. This colony would survive, and they'd get their females back.

When they entered the building, several more scents assailed Chayton. Topping the list were pain and frustration. A table surrounded by ten shifters, male and female, ate up most of the space in the large, square room. Somber expressions greeted the Guardians' arrival.

After they were settled, Chayton folded his hands on the table and eyed the group before speaking to the leader, who mentioned his name was Willem. "Tell me how it went down."

Kaitlyn sat next to him. Her honeysuckle scent grounded him in a familiar way that tightened his gut. He'd sworn himself to another; it didn't matter what the redhead's smell did to him.

He did his best to block her out as the leader spoke.

"They attacked right before dawn when most of the colony were still sleeping. The fires started, diverted us from the real trouble in the development on the outskirts of town."

"Was that where the majority of the casualties took place?" Kaitlyn asked softly.

The leader nodded. "Many of us rushed downtown to put out the fires, leaving our families at home to be attacked. Or worse."

Chayton grimaced. "Do you know anything about the rogues?"

"There'd been sightings." Willem's tone was grave. "No run-ins or encounters, but my people reported there were four rogues. This was the first time we saw them all working together."

One of the colony's females spoke. "We hoped they'd ravage each other in the woods and leave the carcasses to rot."

If they'd been feral, perhaps. Chayton refrained from saying so. Rogues hadn't yet descended into madness and still functioned using higher thinking while shunning society's rules and constraints. Kaitlyn also remained quiet on the point. Members of the colony knew the difference, had chosen to ignore it and paid the price.

Kaitlyn broke the silence. "They weren't recognized as being from any of the packs in your colony?"

Willem shook his head. "No, but this forest is littered with shifter colonies. We're one of the most rural. Beyond us, the terrain becomes too rugged for a decent-sized clan, much less a colony of them."

Except Chayton's home was even deeper into the forest, had been a part of this land for centuries. His people could survive anywhere.

Chapter Three

"We go tonight," Chayton announced. Kaitlyn's eyes flared in an *Aren't we going to discuss this?* silent message. An imperceptible shake of his head answered her. He scanned the faces around the table, who Kaitlyn credited with looking just as wary as she felt.

Fire flashed in Chayton's gaze. "They won't be expecting us and every minute those females are gone is another minute of a nightmare for them."

Yes. She had to agree. The colony's day search had done no good. She and Chayton had no time constraints and didn't need to recover from an attack, like many of the town's leaders.

Kaitlyn stood up. "Be ready to point us toward a healer when we return." She and Chayton weren't returning without them.

From Chayton's surprised glance, he must've expected an argument. She was glad to disappoint.

Willem rose. "We'll send assistance. Patton and Blanche." He inclined his head toward a couple at the back of the room. One of them was the female who spoke.

The male and female exited the building, stripping as they went.

Kaitlyn mentally sighed. This part she hated. Shift, or run? Her ability to shoot better than anyone else and fight hand-to-hand no matter the opponent let her kick ass as a human. But to search deep in the forest, an unfamiliar environment for her, shifting was best. Yet if she found the females and they required aid, all Kaitlyn could do was lick them because the shift back to a human would incapacitate her.

Chayton breezed past her. "Load your stuff in the SUV, we shift and run."

Well, he yanked the decision out of her hands. She just hoped his decision was based on strategy and not spite.

Kaitlyn reached their vehicle and tossed the bag inside. She checked over her shoulder to see the colony's clan leaders peering out of the window and standing on the building's stoop. The two shifters who would accompany them circled further down the street, waiting.

Modesty was another drawback to being raised human. In her pre-shifter days, she'd wear tiny dresses and dance on counters. Stripping down with a male, or two, was totally different than baring all in front of a group.

Chayton ripped his shirt off. His hands worked at his pants and they dropped, too. He kicked them next to the boots he'd shed.

She shut the door and walked around to the other side.

"Seriously?" Chayton muttered.

Kaitlyn refrained from comment and opened the back door. It served two purposes—to fold up her stuff and set it inside, and block herself from Chayton's scrutiny. She removed her boots and shed her clothes as quickly as possible while he gathered his items on the driver's seat. He slammed the door shut, almost jumping her out of her pants.

The whoosh from his shift carried under the door. A hint of desire tainted it. Good. That'd piss him off.

She welcomed the shift as the addicting rush of her animalistic side took over. The world grew brighter, colors more vibrant, smells attacked her nose. Since her first shift, she learned why dogs loved hanging their heads out the windows. Lord, she wished she could shift more. But she had to get past the psychological block and to do that, she'd have to know *why*. What was affecting her so badly she blacked out trying to shift back to human?

Enough about her issues. She had two females to rescue and four rogues to hunt.

Chayton led the other two through Valley Moon. They hung back, knowing he needed to investigate the scents himself to determine where they searched. The female shifter accompanying them, Blanche, pointed out the attackers' scents. Kaitlyn lingered while Chayton filled his nostrils. When it was her turn, she inspected every inch.

There was definitely a difference between normal and batshit crazy shifters. Their scent held a tang like milk ready to sour, or garbage reaching the get-it-out-of-the-house stage.

Three males and one female, all borderline feral. Feral enough to be dangerous, but not so far gone they'd be easy to catch.

Chayton twisted to face them. *Fan out, but follow me. Based on reports, at least two of them were on foot in order to carry the females.*

As they ran toward the trees, Kaitlyn loped to the far right and Chayton the far left. Not that the two assistants weren't excellent trackers, but they weren't Guardians. They could be recruited, put through training, but they'd never be born Guardians like Chayton and Kaitlyn. Her DNA, and her frustrating partner's, was designed for this stuff: increased speed and stamina, stronger tracking skills, extremely heightened senses, and even a special scent that signaled others to their status. Having a Guardian flanking each side expanded their tracking distance.

The farther they got from the colony, the rougher the terrain to navigate and the fainter the scents grew. A benefit to the increased exertion was that each deep breath drew in greater quantities of scent. Progress slowed as they reached a steep embankment.

Blanche spoke first. *This is where we lose their scent, like hitting a wall. I expected that if they shifted back to wolf, the odor would grow stronger, but it just stops.*

Kaitlyn paced up and down, weaving in and out of the trees. Blanche was right. Even the captives' scents were gone. She raised her head to sniff the breeze.

Water? Her communication was for Chayton alone. She trotted to his location while their two assistants circled the area, sniffing for clues.

Yes. A couple rivers run through this part of the state.

Any chance they used the water to cover their tracks?

Chayton's eyes narrowed. He moved forward to crest the embankment and stopped short. Kaitlyn pulled up next to him, but no further. At first glance, the trees they stood in melded with the trees in the horizon—until two feet in front of where she stood. They had topped a short cliff that had been cut into the side of the earth by a fast-flowing river.

A faint rushing noise reached her.

That's a waterfall, Chayton filled in as if he instinctively knew she was unfamiliar with the sound.

She scanned the far side of the river. Lower than the side she was on, it still rose several feet above the water. Studying the riverside, Kaitlyn noticed that each edge of the water had a narrow strip of rocky beach.

It came to her. *They threw them.*

Chayton's head swung toward her. *What?*

~40~

Jutting her snout to the beach, she explained. *See the disrupted rocks at the bottom? The females are shifters, they'll heal. So before they shifted, they tossed them down. Then the attackers jumped into the water from as far back as they could muster.*

His eyes spoke his disbelief.

Only one way to prove it was possible. She trotted back to where their scent cut off.

Don't try it, Savoy, he warned. *I'm not carrying your broken ass back, or parking here and waiting for you to heal.*

The other two shifters sensed distress from Chayton and began pacing around the trees. They hadn't been opened up into their communication yet.

She gauged how much distance she'd need to leap and found a path clear of tree trunks. Crouching low, she dug her claws into the ground and envisioned how this would carry out, one of the many tricks she learned in her years studying martial arts and visualization.

Her claws dug in, her wolf's thighs exploded. She ran as fast as possible and once she reached the area the scent wall hit, she vaulted.

As she flew through the air, she heard the shocked inhales of the male and female. If Kaitlyn didn't crush all her bones with this stunt, would they follow?

She cleared the edge just as her arc rounded to the descent. Her path would end in the water so at least she'd calculated that correctly.

Please be deep enough, please be deep enough.
Dark blue sped toward her, and she hit before the
worry of jagged rocks arose. A giant splash and her
mouth and nose filled with river water. She exhaled
slowly and waited for her downward plunge to end
so she could propel herself to the surface.

When her head broke free, she resisted a howl
of triumph. If she guessed correctly, they would be
back on the hunt.

She glanced up to see Chayton poking his head
over the edge, along with the other two.

He bared his teeth in the wolf version of a
scowl. *Get to shore and see if you can find their
trail.*

Before she exited the water she smelled the
pain from the females. Conscious or not, their
bodies would feel the impact of the rocks. *This is
where they landed.* Kaitlyn sniffed around and faced
downriver, the path the group had taken with their
captives.

A splash startled her. She spun around in time
to see Chayton surface.

He paddled toward her side of the river.
*Blanche and Patton are going to shadow us up on
the ridge.*

Good decision. If either one of them didn't
make the jump, she and Chayton would have to
leave them to mend to finish the search.

They trotted along until the morning's rays
lightened the sky. Fatigue feathered the edges of
Kaitlyn's mind, but she blocked it out. The little

discomfort she experienced was nothing like what the captured females suffered.

They split their time between the rocks and the water to save their paws. The trails grew clearer, as if the rogues worried less that they'd be followed over time. The cliff eventually dwindled until it was only feet above water level. Blanche and Patton stayed on shore, letting Chayton lead.

Miles went by. Her stomach rumbled, but she ignored it. They were closing in.

A distant howl sounded. Spurred by the noise, they ran faster. The rushing sound grew louder until they found themselves at the edge of the rapids and the trail evaporated.

Chayton nosed the river's edge. *They probably went back to higher ground.*

Nothing over here, Patton answered. *Did they cross to the other side?*

It'd make sense, Chayton answered.

Gingerly, Kaitlyn picked her way over the rocks that preceded the rapids. Cold water swirled around her legs with a force that could topple her in where she'd be battered by the rapids. When she was close enough, she leapt to the riverbank. A sickening smell assaulted her: death.

Chayton landed behind her. *Shit.*

The other two shifters picked their way across more slowly than the Guardians, but she waited for them. Understanding dawned on their faces. She led them to where Chayton located the body of a naked and beaten female. The way she'd been beheaded sat like lead in Kaitlyn's gut.

That's Shelly, Blanche said. Even mentally, Kaitlyn heard the pang of loss in her words.

Chayton searched the surrounding areas. *She fought too much. They couldn't keep her without risking themselves.*

That's Shelly, Blanche said again, pride lifting her tone. *She always fought hard before being made to do something she didn't want to.*

Kaitlyn's assessing gaze swept the woman's body. The rogues had forced themselves on her. The smell of sexual assault bombarded Kaitlyn's senses until she choked back bile. She didn't know if the others smelled it, or guessed at it, but for Kaitlyn the unique mixture of blood, semen, domination, and pain couldn't be missed.

She directed her communication to Chayton. *She was raped before they killed her.*

That's what the rogues took her for. The female in their pack probably tires of servicing them. His tone held the same urgency at finding the pack to save the other female.

When we find Terri, Blanche said solemnly.

Patton nodded. *We'll carry Shelly's body back for a proper burial.*

Of course, Chayton answered. He detected the trail again and took off. Their efforts were infused with the drive to find the rogues before Terri met the same fate. They traversed the countryside until voices drifted to them on the wind. Chayton slowed, his movements precise and quiet.

Kaitlyn unconsciously mimicked him. Stalking was instinctive, but she didn't spend as much time in her wolf form as Chayton. He flowed through the environment not like he was a part of it, but like the world moved around him.

Growls and yips grew louder.

"Shift, dammit," a male's guttural voice demanded.

Kaitlyn paused, but Chayton kept his progress moving forward.

The wolf in distress was female. Terri?

"I'll shift back and take you like a dog," the male snarled. "You're a fool if you think it doesn't matter."

A female's voice spoke with sinister humor. "You already proved that to the other one."

"Maybe I should shoot her in the leg." This from another male who sounded bored. "Take some of the fight out of her for a few hours."

Chayton's voice floated through her mind. *We're downwind. You and I sneak as close as we can. They have at least one gun. We take the armed ones down first. Blanche, Patton, hang back until we attack, then get in and save the female.*

The two shifters communicated their understanding.

Chayton eased forward and stopped. She pulled up next to him and surveyed the scene.

The four rogues in their naked human form surrounded Terri. A fair-haired male whose skin was dotted with freckles pointed a shotgun toward her.

Kaitlyn's head spun and her vision blurred for a moment. What the hell? She wasn't shifting back, why'd she feel like she was going to pass out? She shook off the sensation.

Wait for my signal, Chayton ordered.

A third man kicked the wolf. She yelped in pain, and Kaitlyn barely bit back a growl.

Wait. Chayton glanced at her out of the corner of his eye.

You don't have to worry about me. Like she was impulsive enough to mess up this mission after they'd trekked miles and miles.

She breathed calmly through his loaded silence lest she signal their presence by her massive spike of vexation.

"We need to keep moving," the female rogue said. "You shouldn't have let her heal well enough to fight. She's slowing us down."

"Sida, you're such a fucking downer." The male with the shotgun tapped Terri's flank. She spun and bared her fangs. "Shift."

Terri snapped at the barrel of the gun. The male's expression didn't change when he swung the barrel to catch her in the jaw. Her head was flung back. The crack of bone made Kaitlyn's blood boil. Next to her, Chayton stood, ready to attack, but as seemingly unaffected as if he'd watched them doing the waltz.

Kaitlyn's gaze riveted on the fair-haired male. Something about him revolted her, other than his rogue behavior. She couldn't quite pinpoint it. And the way he held that gun with a cruel glare…

Terri lunged to attack the male, but he grinned as the other three jumped her before she reached him.

You take the lone male. Now! Chayton bounded into the melee, Kaitlyn hot on his heels. He landed on the topmost shifter, one of the males, and sunk his teeth into a hamstring.

The male's yell rang out as the one brandishing the shotgun shouted, "*Guardians!*" He swung his gun up to aim at Chayton.

Kaitlyn leapt, knocking it off target as the boom rang out. The world momentarily muted from the blast firing next to her ears. She chomped down on the male's trigger arm. He snarled in pain and rage, his other fist beating at her as he stumbled back.

His strength astonished her. The brain chemistry of rogues and ferals changed, much like someone high on meth. And he knew it.

His fist rained down on her, but he wouldn't drop the gun. She wanted to gag on his sour blood, but she'd lose her grip. Barks and howls told Kaitlyn that Blanche and Patton had joined in to rescue Terri.

The fair-haired male swung around with Kaitlyn still attached. She danced on her hind legs, whipping her head back and forth until his bones ground against her teeth. It'd take a whole river to wash the gross tang out of her mouth.

Despite their jerky movements, he landed several solid blows on her side. Ribs cracked and pain blossomed over her back. She'd have to let go and use another route of attack.

During their spin, her back paws tripped over someone else's legs. Her jaw disengaged as she struggled to right herself but ended up crashing to her belly. The limbs that had felled her belonged to an unconscious Terri, whose sweat-clumped hair draped over a pale face.

Kaitlyn swung her head up to face the gun-wielding male, the image of Terri branded in her mind. The male's hard stare pinned both of them and he raised the gun.

Oh god. Kaitlyn's world slowed. An unconscious, defenseless woman and Kaitlyn looking up at a male determined to hurt them both. Déjà vu slammed into her.

Oh god. She'd been through this before. Her world spun. She shook her head and heard the male chuckle.

Rage filled her, but instead of fueling her, her world dimmed. She was out before her nose slammed into the ground.

In his peripheral vision, Chayton saw Kaitlyn crumple completely and shift back to creamy skin. He loosened his jaw from around a dark-haired shifter's ankle and jumped to defend her from the blond shifter who repeatedly kicked her prone form. Chayton sailed over the prostrate Terri to tackle the man assaulting Kaitlyn.

In his rational mind, he cursed himself. How dare he leave a victim to save a Guardian? The mission came first. Any Guardian would expect their partner to save the helpless, even if they were incapacitated themselves.

The male sidestepped. He cradled the shotgun in his good arm while his other hand hung in a bloodied, dripping mess at his side. A flash of metal preceded another boom, this one aimed in Chayton's direction.

Heat seared through his back right leg. It wasn't a direct hit, but enough to pepper his extremity with tiny granules of torture. For a heartbeat after the blast, everything quieted. The eruption of growls and barks behind him meant the other rogues had shifted to fight Blanche and Patton.

Chayton ignored the agony in his hindquarters to lunge at the male, who shifted and met Chayton in midair. Chayton blocked out the fire of teeth tearing at his hide as he tried to subdue the shifter, but couldn't latch on to the male's neck. When Chayton could glance at the dogpile, he saw his two helpers losing ground. The rogues exploited the unconscious Guardian and Terri.

A deep howl blasted through the trees. The rogues flinched and broke apart from the fight. The way their eyes darted back and forth, they were communicating mentally.

Abruptly, they all turned and sped away as fast as their four legs could go. The lightest wolf was the slowest, from the damage Kaitlyn had caused. Chayton strained to run after them. Patton and Blanche would care for the females, but he couldn't leave Kaitlyn's side.

He had to pursue. His nature, his job, was to destroy the rogues. He sprinted several yards, and kicked up dirt when he skidded to a stop.

The howl sounded again, but closer. The enemy of his enemy may not be his friend. Chayton needed to stick around to cover the others from the unknown shifter approaching.

Blanche stood point, facing into the trees like Chayton. Patton hovered over the downed females.

The shifter stepped from the copse and he wasn't a typical shifter. He stood on two legs like a man, but had a lightly furred torso and a shaggy mane of fur around his neck. He was the same shifter he and Kaitlyn had encountered earlier.

It's the ancient one, Cian. Blanche visibly relaxed. *He will not harm us. He is…he's not quite right in the head, even for an ancient.*

Ancient. No wonder the male's scent had registered as oddly familiar. A small amount of similarity to his *ahte's* scent.

No menace radiated off the large humanoid wolf. He kept his distance, his keen gaze on the females.

A groan and rustling captured all of their attention. Terri sat up with a gasp, shoving hair out of her eyes. The cascade of emotions flipping across her face dug into Chayton's gut. Confusion, followed by panic, then rage, and when she realized she was surrounded by clan members and Guardians, relieved sorrow. She drew her feet up to herself as her gaze landed on Kaitlyn. When she saw the rest were in wolf form, she transitioned.

Are they dead, Terri asked, her tone hopeful.

No, Chayton answered. *I will hunt them after I care for my partner.*

They all stared at Kaitlyn. Her long, toned body starkly contrasted with the green and brown earth. Her coppery hair was freed from its braid and splayed around her, covering her face and shoulders. Besides the angry red welts across her ribs, she didn't appear injured in any other way. She wasn't an idiot. She wouldn't have tried shifting in the middle of a fight, not with her history of passing out.

Chayton addressed Terri first. *Do you think you can travel back to the colony?*

Yes. Her answer was firm, resolved. She might be weakened, traumatized, but she wasn't empty of fight.

Are you okay with your clan members leading you back? Chayton wasn't going to make the female go anywhere with anyone she didn't want to.

Terri inclined her head.

Leave the remains of Shelly. We'll carry her back to the colony. The rogues were still out there and they had Terri to protect.

I will return Shelly to her family. She was in my pack. Patton threaded his way through the trees, taking lead as if sensing Terri didn't want a male where she couldn't see him. Blanche hung back so Terri was effectively sandwiched between them.

Chayton didn't argue. He wouldn't take the honor from the male.

Kaitlyn's legs twitched, drawing his stare to her lush, rounded bottom. Why'd he have to be here with her? He needed to convince the commander to switch her out with another Guardian. One of them had to be freed up by now.

He lifted his gaze to the ancient, sensing only curiosity. *What do you seek?*

The female. Is she well?

If the ancient had a history with the colony, perhaps he knew Terri.

Chayton glanced in the direction the other shifters had gone. *She'll recover.*

Not her. The Guardian.

A low rumble of a growl escaped Chayton. Why was the male inquiring after his…Kaitlyn? *She's fine.*

The ancient studied him, like Chayton's soul was bared. Another similarity with Chayton's father. The males had once been superior to modern shifters. Now, Chayton wondered if the purpose of life was escaping them.

Cian turned and trotted away, but he didn't go far. Perhaps he knew Chayton still sensed his presence and didn't care.

Kaitlyn's awareness flipped on like a switch. Chayton waited with mild annoyance as she twisted and jumped to her feet, frantically looking around. When she saw no one else, she gulped and turned her attention to him. Bright spots highlighted her cheeks once she realized she stood nude before him.

What a sight. Her body was a masterpiece. It took serious effort to hold his gaze on her face. Desire had no place in dealing with what had just happened.

Her intention to shift showed in her expression.

Don't you dare shift. He may have mentally shouted his command.

She winced and put her hand to her head.

Allowing calm to take over, he flowed into his human form with his braids gone, his ink-black hair draped across his shoulders. Kaitlyn's blush deepened and she glanced away.

"What happened?" She scanned their surroundings, but he knew she was avoiding him.

His anger spiked. "You *passed out*, that's what happened. We had to protect your sleeping ass while handing our own over to *four* nearly feral shifters. If that fucking ancient hadn't howled and scared them shitless, I honestly don't know how this situation would've ended."

Her jaw worked and her eyes glistened. She was fighting tears. He should've felt like a jackass for tearing into her, but it wasn't only anger fueling his reaction. The thought of her getting hurt tore him apart inside.

He directed his next question to the area of the forest that Cian watched them from. "If they're so scared of you, and the colony is full of adoring fans, why haven't you killed those rogues?"

Silence.

"Glad to see ancient morals are alive and strong." Chayton huffed and pushed his hair away from his face.

Kaitlyn was also peering at where Cian hid. Of course she could tell he was there, just like she'd spotted him the first time. What was it with her and this ancient? Had they met before?

"I think I had a flashback." Kaitlyn pulled her attention to him, her eyes anchored to his face just like his were to hers. "I think…I have an idea why I have trouble shifting. Or at least where it originated from." She blinked rapidly and pressed her fingers to her temples.

He wanted to snap at her, but she spoke softly, seemed distressed. If she passed out again, he'd either have to perch next to her naked body or carry it. He didn't dare let that idea take root. Kaitlyn didn't suspect his feelings toward her and he wasn't going to broadcast them with an erection.

"Talk and walk, Cinnamon." Chayton did just that, not waiting for Kaitlyn to follow.

They covered a few hundred yards before Kaitlyn continued. "My dad killed my mom."

He cut a surprised look over his shoulder that she was going to talk about it and slowed enough that she pulled even with him.

"He was super controlling, obsessed with Mom, but he loved us. We had good days and bad days. Life was normal, nothing different from any of my friends." She absentmindedly pulled all her hair over one shoulder, letting her fingers work through it. "During the struggle with the rogue, I fell over Terri. She lay so pale, so still. Then I looked up at him, standing over us with his gun."

She fell quiet. Birds paused in their singing as they passed. They hiked and scrambled through the trees. Their feet were dirty and torn navigating the terrain. Two legs were so much slower than four. Sweat dotted his brow despite the coolness of the day. He missed his braids with his unbound hair acting like a thermal blanket over his back.

"I've seen that look before," she continued. "I've seen it all before. And I've seen it all from the perspective of a wolf, but I don't remember that night."

"You were there?" That would begin to explain some of her issues. He'd heard she was adopted by humans, but not why.

"Yes." Her expression was pensive. "I woke to—" she dipped her head with a grimace like her lingering headache had flared "—police banging on the door. I guess the neighbors called the cops after they heard the gunshots. I was naked, lying next to my mom, and my dad…" She drifted again. "That rogue resembled him." She sighed. "Dad shot himself after he killed Mom. I think I witnessed it all, and I think I was in my shifter form."

"Your mom wasn't a shifter?"

Kaitlyn shook her head. "Not that I remember. Dad wasn't either."

"One of them had to be." A simple gunshot wouldn't kill a shifter.

Her stricken expression dented his resentment. He'd given her so much shit for being raised human, but it's not like she'd had any control over it. Like him, she was piecing together that one of her parents may not have donated part of her genetic material.

She coughed in an attempt to cover up a sniffle. "I don't remember shifting—ever—before the night the Guardians helped me out. The two men I had partied with tried to kill me. I shifted and ripped them apart. I was kind of a mess after that."

He held back a growl. It was a good thing they were dead then. "Not remembering you shifted doesn't mean you never had. Were your parents together when you were born?" *When you were conceived?*

She read into his question. "As far as I know. Dad was the jealous type. He and Mom always fought about where she'd been and how long she'd taken, but he must've had no reason to think I wasn't his. I'm the spitting image of my mom, so if one of my parents isn't my birth parent, then it's Dad. Mom must've strayed."

Sweet Mother, Kaitlyn looked miserable. She wasn't holding tears back any longer, but seemed too numb to cry.

"After the cops came through, then what?" He had to know the rest of the story, had to know everything he could about Kaitlyn.

Her expression turned disgusted. "They tested me for sexual assault. I mean, I didn't know why I was naked either, but Dad wasn't like that. He wouldn't have hurt me." Again she blinked rapidly and shook her head like she was fending off another blackout. "I think that's why I was still alive. He couldn't kill me, just stormed to his bedroom, dug out his pistol, shot himself. That's the police report, anyway. Like I said, I don't remember, probably had passed out already. My mom's sister and her husband adopted me."

He didn't want to keep pushing—she was obviously destroyed. Even his libido shut down around her mental torment and she was walking buck-naked next to him. "Did you sense anything about your aunt and uncle having any shifting abilities?"

"Nope."

So Kaitlyn's abilities came from her dad's side. And the dad she knew probably wasn't her real dad. Shifter healing abilities made it difficult to commit suicide.

She rubbed her forehead. "Can we shift and run back? I can shift at the edge of town and as I come to, you can head in and talk to the colony."

Like he'd leave her naked ass out cold in the forest where rogues and weird ancients ran? "We'll figure it out when we get there." He flowed into his wolf and Kaitlyn did the same.

Chapter Four

Kaitlyn sat on the bed in the small motel room with her elbows resting on her knees, head hanging.

What a terrible day. Night had fallen and she was running on no sleep. Well, other than her nap on the forest floor. Fatigue dragged at her. She'd be humiliated if it wasn't for the flashbacks. Sometimes images visited her in her sleep, but never in Technicolor like earlier. Never with the full play-by-play.

A hot tear slid down her cheek. Ugh, she hated crying. It had frayed her nerves trying to hold it together around Chayton. It would've helped if he'd been his normal self, but he'd listened, although she sensed his upset at stopping pursuit of the rogues for her. She wished he hadn't.

The ancient who'd shadowed them all the way to the colony had intentions to protect that were almost palpable. No hostility, no hidden agenda, he just watched over them. Why her and Chayton when Cian survived in his own little world?

Chayton. After she'd awoken from her shift back, she'd found him with his back to her, keeping watch, his emotions carefully concealed, fortified by steady breathing, almost like meditation. They marched into town in silence and quickly dressed. More people had seen Kaitlyn naked today than she cared for, but she had to admit how freeing it was. Shifters didn't possess human mental limitations about nudity.

However, being around a naked male who was her destined mate left her in a state of confused need. Chayton asked Blanche to set Kaitlyn up in a room while he went with Willem to conference call Commander Fitzsimmons—after Chayton briefed their boss on what happened. Kaitlyn hated missing out on the information, but the commander was aware of her liability, he'd understand. Chayton said he'd swing by and update her.

With a sigh, she stretched out on the bed. She wore shorts and a T-shirt, all her gear was laid out and ready to go when Chayton gave the order. There was nothing for her to do. Her eyelids drifted shut and sleep came in a cloud of darkness that dissipated to leave an image. A dream that uncloaked her memories.

Her father stood over her, his expression tormented. Kaitlyn marveled at the sharpness in the world as her heart crashed against her ribs.

What just happened? She'd been unusually crabby the entire week. Mom had made a million hormone comments and sure enough, her period—first one ever—had started. Kaitlyn had rushed out to grab her mom and then…everything went dark.

Her T-shirt was hanging off her neck. She shook out of it. The room looked different. Everything smelled different.

A scream. Her mom's fear tasted bitter, like orange peel. Her father's spike of shock. The closet door opened and the tang of metal and gunpowder caused her to sneeze.

It was all so clear, but overlaid with the haziness of the dream world. Kaitlyn's gaze dropped down. She had paws!

"What is *that*, Maxine?" Mind-bending confusion rocked Dad's voice. His accusing eyes shot from Kaitlyn's mom to her.

"Don't shoot it. It's Kaitlyn."

The shotgun shook in his hands.

He stabbed his hand through his hair, the wildness in his eyes almost frantic. "My kid shouldn't turn into *that*."

"She's just—she's just a child. Don't hurt her." Mom's voice shook. Kaitlyn had never seen her so scared, not even during arguments with Dad.

The barrel swung to aim at her face. Kaitlyn whined.

"That's not real. It can't be." But he'd been there, standing next to her mom when it'd happened. Her clothing was scattered around her.

Mom crept closer to Dad, hands outstretched toward the gun. "Unless we're all hallucinating, this thing is Kaitlyn."

He barked out a hard laugh. "Who'd you fuck that turns into a wolf?"

His eyes widened when he realized his question wasn't rhetorical. Mom shook her head but her denial came too late. In her eyes was panic that she was caught in a lie and they'd both suffer.

His voice dropped to barely audible, personal anguish resided in his expression. "She's not...she's not mine?"

Kaitlyn whimpered, snagging his attention. She watched disbelief fade to resignation. She tried to say something, but only yips escaped.

Darkness descended over his craggy features, and his resolute gaze slid over to her mother. "I knew I couldn't trust you."

Mom's mouth dropped in horror.

Dad? She couldn't form words.

With aching clarity, the shotgun barrel swung. Kaitlyn's mom ducked, but the blast beat her. Kaitlyn flinched, momentarily deafened. Mom's crumpled body lay feet away, shock frozen upon her youthful face. The thick stench of blood staining her clothing assaulted Kaitlyn. A thick stench of blood assaulted her. Her gaze lifted to her dad.

He was the calm center as the world swirled behind him. The loss in his eyes staggered her. She whined, but the noise only anchored his acceptance that she wasn't his.

The barrel swayed back to her. She shifted and shook her head, her way of begging him not to hurt her. His gaze slid to her mother's body. There was no fooling herself anymore. She smelled death.

Mom was gone and Dad wanted to kill her. Kaitlyn's breathing picked up. The sound of her panting filled the room. Quick shallow breaths did nothing to stop the room from spinning.

A disgusted noise escaped from Dad, a sob tore from his throat. Kaitlyn wanted to go to him, get a hug, have him tell her it'd be all right. Instead, he dropped the shotgun and trudged to the master bedroom. The droop in his shoulders, the shuffling of his footsteps shredded Kaitlyn. He was the strong one, sometimes scaring her in his dedication to his family. She should hate him, wish for hell to swallow him up because he'd taken her mother away, but…he was all she had left. He was her dad and she loved him.

She stood to go after to him, but the door slammed. After a moment, she padded over to her mother's body. Mom's pale face, her unmoving limbs, her vitality drained from her body… Kaitlyn shook her head as the dizziness descended.

When a gunshot echoed from the bedroom, it was like the sound punched a hole in her brain and darkness took over.

"Kaitlyn?" A hand patted her shoulder.

Kaitlyn readjusted herself in bed. This wasn't like her memory. The police had jostled her to rouse her. They'd been talking rapidly amongst themselves, speculating about what happened. None of them had said her name, and it hadn't smelled like beef stew.

"Kaitlyn?" The pats turned to firm rubs.

Her eyes flew open; she was fully awake. Her gaze met Chayton's concerned one.

He leaned back on the bed where he perched on the edge next to her. "Sweet Mother, finally. I've been trying to wake you for ten minutes."

She sat up with a frown. To-go containers sat on the nightstand. Her stomach rumbled. "I was dreaming, only it was my memory. Everything I hadn't remembered until tonight."

Rubbing her eyes, she noticed how close her position brought her to Chayton. She couldn't move away. The heat emanating off of him, his fresh-cut pine scent brought her too much comfort to distance herself.

"What'd your dream tell you?" His voice was soft, his hand twitched like he wanted to touch her somehow.

"What we already suspected. Only it clarified that my dad's not my dad and my mom cheated on him." She chuckled sadly. "Not the kind of drama I thought was behind my condition."

"Did your mom know your biological father was a shifter?"

"I don't know. She seemed as shocked as Dad that I turned into a wolf." Then Kaitlyn had sensed her mother's *he's going to find out* vibe. "You know what's fucked up? I was never mad at Dad. Maybe for a little bit, but I was always disappointed in him for what he did. Sad that the man I thought was our rock was so weak he was compelled to kill Mom and run away by killing himself." She fiddled with her fingernails. "But now I'm so pissed at both of them."

Chayton studied her. "Perhaps your mom understood his instability and that's why she couldn't leave him." He pushed a strand of her hair behind her ear. "You know. We see it all the time in our work. One half of the couple is afraid to leave. It's all they know or they fear physical harm."

Asshole Chayton she could handle. Compassionate Chayton scrambled her good sense. And she wanted comfort. The last several hours turned her world upside down.

He leaned his head down, she tilted her face to meet his. When their lips touched, lightning flashed through her body. He inhaled sharply, but didn't break contact. One hand cradled her face, the other slid around her waist to draw her closer.

She deepened the kiss, wanted him to carry her to another place where she didn't have to think about her messed-up past. He growled. His tongue swiped across her lips and she opened for him. Together they fell back onto the bed and he shifted until he stretched out over her.

The way his body blanketed her, his heat seeping into her cold spirit, soothed her. Tampered the turmoil remaining from her dream. She parted her legs to cradle him. His growing erection pressed against her lower belly. Any unease left from her dream was wiped away. Oh yeah, she'd seen him naked, knew his impressive size, but hadn't experienced it fully aroused. She ached to have him inside. Instinctively, she knew he'd be all she needed. Before, she had to seek out more than one partner to give her some semblance of satisfaction, but the male on top of her promised complete fulfillment.

Her hands stroked his broad shoulders, followed his shoulder holster down around his back. His muscles rippled under her fingers as he rocked against her core.

She moaned her approval, her hips meeting his. His touch lit her on fire. He lifted himself enough to be able to cup her breasts. She'd gone braless after her shower, thank goodness, but she cursed the barrier her shirt created between their skins.

The fall of jet black hair encompassed her completely in his scent and acted like a wall between them and the outside world. She dragged her hands up his back to bury them into his soft hair. He ripped his lips away to trail kisses along her neck as his touch traveled down until his fingers skimmed the waistband of her shorts.

"Yes, Chay, please."

At her shortened version of his name, he nipped the tender skin of her neck in approval. She fisted his hair and surged up to rub along the sizeable ridge in his pants. If his mouth hadn't been doing wicked things to her, she'd want to peek, sure the tip of shaft pushed past the waist of his pants. She wondered if the head glistened as wet as she had grown.

The band of her shorts lifted and his fingers found her center.

She threw her head back with a gasp. "I need more."

He rubbed circles with his thumb on her clit until her entire focus was on that bundle of nerves. Dimly, she was aware of him kissing her neck, but when he tunneled one finger inside, her core became her only focus.

This one male did more to her with his mouth and one hand than any other she'd been with. How she wished she could strip him down, or even take his shirt off, but she was helpless with what he was doing to her.

He threaded another finger inside and pumped them in and out.

"Chay," she gasped, "I can't—I can't hold it off. Oh god, I'm going to come so hard."

She crested the peak with a low moan. He worked her center, pushing her over the edge. Shuddering and quaking around him, she thought her heart would stop when his mouth opened against the base of her neck. His fangs pricked her skin. The sensation increased the power of her orgasm tenfold.

"Yes, yes," she encouraged him, riding out her release and hugging him tightly to her.

His head jerked up with a grimace, his eyes wide with shock. Tension radiated from him as he held his body statue-still.

Something was wrong. She collapsed against the bed, but cradled his face in her hands.

"Chay, what's wrong?" He hadn't said a word since before they kissed. Female pride that she'd carried him away was pushed out by dismay at his reaction.

He shoved off her. Horror dawned in his eyes. "This can't happen again, Savoy."

She flinched like he'd slapped her. Savoy? He got her off and that didn't even earn her a "Cinnamon"?

How naïve was she? She thought he'd come around for her, his mate.

She sat up, scowling at him. "Well, I didn't ask for it in the first place."

He stalked to the door. "I almost marked you. I can't believe it."

He dreaded everyone knowing she belonged to him that badly?

"Why? Because it's so horrible that I was raised human?" She stood up, ready to shove him out of the door.

He stiffened and paused. "Yeah, that's it. I can't be with someone who can't be fully in touch with their wolf. It's a disgrace."

Her gasp startled even her. Yet as he stormed out of the room, she caught the slight whiff of a lie.

***

Chayton finished packing his duffle and zipped it shut. He stood over it, unmoving, dreading what came next. He had to meet Kaitlyn outside in a few minutes.

How was he going to face her? It was hard to maintain scorn when her body lifted him to heights he'd never known existed. And they hadn't even had sex. She was so responsive, he had felt…needed. A powerful feeling from someone as strong and independent as Kaitlyn.

He'd come back to his room and washed her scent off of him. He had to. His body was primed to ignite if she even looked at him. Sitting in his room with a raging erection and her arousal covering him spelled out disaster. One that'd end with him begging at her door. She'd likely kick him in his engorged shaft and he'd deserve it.

Disgrace. Had he actually called her that?

Yes, he had, and he needed to remember why. He'd promised himself to Tika. Her family wouldn't allow him to back out, not when her mother had insisted on a blood oath. He wouldn't dishonor his father, the only family he had left. Chayton's bloodline must be preserved. Tika's ancient blood wasn't as pure as his, but her grandfather had been an ancient, and more importantly, her father had come from the same tribe as Chayton's mother.

Tika. He pictured her doe-brown eyes and lively smile. No physical reaction. He'd managed passion with her before, last year when he'd stopped home between Guardian assignments. Her father pushed for their union, but Chayton remained firm in waiting until Tika was at least a quarter century old. He'd run with her in the woods, one thing led to another, and…at least they were physically compatible. Or so he had thought until his encounter with Kaitlyn. Because now his time with Tika was fuzzy and what he remembered was a watered-down version of the act of sex. Nothing nearly as powerful as the taste he'd had of his mate.

Mate. Kick that idea out of his head. *Tika* was his mate. Not by destiny, but by choice. In less than a couple hours, he'd have to face that choice as he and Kaitlyn were ordered to head to his colony.

Commander Fitzsimmons thought, along with Chayton, that the rogues would target another town. Unfortunately, the closest one was Chayton's colony. The commander wanted them to check in with the leader and then search the forest for the four rogues.

A knock on his door startled him out of his introspection.

"Hurry up, Eagle." Kaitlyn sounded as pissed as she should be.

He'd texted her the commander's orders and apparently, she was ready. He was, too. Willem had been briefed and the commander was giving Spirit Moon a heads up.

Walking out into the daylight, he met Kaitlyn's frosty gaze.

He inclined his head to the SUV. "Get in."

"You have the keys." Her tone could freeze a lake.

The lock popped up when he hit the fob. She spun to throw her stuff in the backseat. No doors were slammed. Her movements were sharp, purposeful. He tossed his gear next to hers and climbed in.

The drive to his colony was silent. Two hours of frigid company watching trees go by. Eight thousand times he'd wanted to say something, but what? *Sorry I promised myself to someone else and made you feel like shit to take the sting off?*

As soon as he'd laid eyes on Kaitlyn for the first time and that unfamiliar feeling of possessiveness swept through him, he'd cursed Tika's father. The proud, confident male had assured Chayton he wouldn't cross paths with his mate; therefore, bonding himself to Tika interfered with nothing. Chayton had been in a bad headspace after the fire that claimed his mother, so he'd caved.

Chayton couldn't renege on his deal with Tika's father. He wouldn't be able to face his own father in doing so. Claiming his human-raised mate who had neither ancient blood nor Sioux blood would make him the disgrace. And having her pass out in front of them after a shift…unthinkable.

Forget their fathers. Tika's mother would rip his throat out and shred his privates. At this point, he'd relish his junk getting trashed. He'd decided to honor Tika after their weekend together and not lie with anyone else. But since Kaitlyn and her

~71~

torturous honeysuckle scent crossed his path, he'd been in a constant state of painful arousal. Last night, his discomfort exceeded bounds no normal male should ever tolerate.

Aaand he would cut off that line of thinking before he clogged the cab with arousal. Angry Kaitlyn's chances at surviving his colony with any pride or sense of self intact were better than a hurt and confused Kaitlyn.

He hated himself for messing with her emotions. Even if he found her girlish exuberance annoying…and refreshing…and hotter than hell.

No, it'd be easier if she disliked him.

A town appeared around the curve. Spread out in the valley were small houses that'd blend into any American town. Along the hillside, dwellings dotted the landscape. Some were log cabins, some stick-built, but all of them were built on a foundation of pride and hard work. The last two hundred years had brought many changes to Spirit Moon, but his people ensured they blended no matter what.

He let off the gas. The highway transformed into Main Street. Two-story brick buildings lined each side. Aside from a gas station or bank, good luck expecting to find a chain store in Spirit Moon. His people were fiercely independent, even in business.

Part of him tuned in to Kaitlyn's reaction to his home. She sat a little straighter, a trace of awe in her expression. She wouldn't dignify him with amazement or appreciation, not after how he'd treated her. Regardless, something deep down in him didn't want her to disapprove of his home, or almost as bad, not be impressed.

"The Guardians never have to come here, do they?" She still didn't look at him, but she fiddled with the braid resting over her right shoulder.

He'd fantasized too many times about that hair draped over his bare skin. "No. We take care of our own."

"So do other colonies, but they know that some issues are strictly in Guardian territory."

He heard her censure. She might be right, be she didn't understand the backbone that lined his people. "My people are honorable and loyal. Anarchy is not a concern."

She passed him a droll look. "You might think so, but it's never one hundred percent. The commander hasn't expressed any concern over a colony that never utilizes our services and stays out of shifter government? And if they didn't have anything to do with the old governing body, how'd they feel about vampires and shifters uniting to govern all the non-humans?"

Yeah, that hadn't gone over well. "They took it in stride."

Has the weakness spread that far? Like hell we'll ever cooperate with a fanger. Those were the kindest words Mato had to say. As colony leader, he'd received the news diplomatically and then ignored it. *We take care of our own*. They'd do as they'd always done. Mato's word was law, and he happened to be Tika's father.

Chayton's father took the road of apathy. The male had lost his mate and not gone crazy, so a little government shake-up was nothing in the grand scheme of things. But he didn't hold the power like Mato.

"The boss briefed them on our arrival?" She was back in work mode. Her conversation clinical.

"Yes." It'd give them time to assemble and the news of Guardian interference would go over better coming from the commander. Mato was old enough to still treat Chayton like a young boy whose balls hadn't dropped yet.

Chayton wished they hadn't. The lingering ache from remaining constantly unsatisfied reminded him that he'd not released himself with Kaitlyn. Not even in the shower, where it felt like a betrayal to seek pleasure, or at least ease his discomfort, when he'd said what he did to her. Not to mention the niggling guilt from having sworn himself to loyalty with Tika.

No one waited outside of the early nineteenth-century house he pulled to a stop in front of. It was situated on Main Street with a manicured lawn of grass that'd turned brown with the approach of winter. Neatly trimmed bushes rimmed the front porch that crossed the entire front of the house. The roof was tipped with several peaks, the windows decorated with tidy white shutters, and two strong columns bordered the entrance. During its time, it'd been a mansion, but it was still a good-sized house.

Mato's house.

Tika lived a few blocks away and Chayton hoped she stayed home. Even better—that she hadn't heard of his visit.

Kaitlyn exited the SUV first, not waiting for Chayton's approval. Not that she needed it, but he preferred to buffer her from his colony's scrutiny.

Without revealing his haste, he used his long legs to quickly catch up and pass her before they reached the door. It swung open to reveal a willowy beauty whose face was gently lined with creases, the only hints that belied her age.

Mato's mate, Zitkana, smiled at him. "Chayton, welcome."

She was normally solemn, but he detected the tension under her expression. Her eyes flicked from him to Kaitlyn, who waited behind him with her hands folded together in front of her in a respectful fashion. Some Guardians liked to storm in, swinging their authority around. That was his preferred method. Others chose a passive route because it also led to a lowering of defenses if their arrival was less than welcome.

"Zitkana," he greeted warmly. He leaned in to kiss each side of her face.

The older shifter gave him a brief hug and spun to lead them inside. "Mato is finishing up some colony business. Your father is already here."

Chayton schooled his expression and breathed an air of calmness through his body lest they scent his nervousness. The floor creaked and their steps echoed through the house. He did nothing to prevent it. Zitkana's light steps hardly made a sound and Kaitlyn was skilled enough to not make a racket, but she again chose to be passive, letting the noise announce their arrival. A tendril of admiration wove through him. With her fighting expertise, she could swagger through town touting her right to be there and she'd have the ability to back up her claim. Instead, she took the road of diplomacy, which also happened to be the key to underestimation, something he was more than guilty of when it came to her.

A male's voice rose to a shout. "We need to open up business with a supplier, Mato. We can get materials for the warehouse at wholesale instead of driving hours to Freemont several times a year."

Zitkana slowed and threw an *I'm sorry, it might be a few minutes* look over her shoulder.

Mato answered. "I said no. It opens our people to too much risk."

"It'd be one delivery a month, maybe even just a quarter. We need to update with the times. We need to save money—"

"No."

"I swear, Mato," the male's voice deepened, "you will regret the iron rule you use with us."

"You've been saying that for so many years, all I hear any more is hot air wasting space." Mato's words dripped with arrogance. "Get out. You waste my time with this nonsense."

They were almost to the door when an angry male stormed past them, his face a mask of fury. Thomas. Some things never changed. Whenever Chayton came to town, those two were always arguing over something.

"Chayton." Mato's low rumble expressed nothing of his mood. He'd probably blown off the confrontation with his clan leaders before Thomas had slammed the front door.

Chayton inclined his head in greeting to the elder shifter before turning to his father. His *ahte* was centuries older than Mato, but to a human, he'd look decades younger. Only the deeply rooted view of pain in his father's eyes and the knowing look he gave everyone suggested he was much older than he appeared.

"This is my partner, Kaitlyn." Chayton gestured to Kaitlyn to take a seat as he addressed her. "This is the colony leader, Mato, and my *ahte*, Des."

Mato dismissed her, but *Ahte* narrowed his gaze on her in curiosity.

When he reached the table the males sat around, Chayton resisted pulling out a chair for Kaitlyn. Now more than ever, he needed to make it appear as if their association with each other went no further than business. He worried that if the formidable leader found out she was Chayton's destined mate, that her life would be in danger. He was overreacting, but something in his gut said to proceed with caution and he was old enough to never ignore it.

With the two powerful males in the room, it was unmistakable who was in charge. His *ahte* reclined in his seat with a couldn't care less look and dressed down. Neat and tidy, but comfortable and versatile. Worn jeans and a buttoned-up work shirt, he'd blend anywhere. While Mato wore his salt-and-pepper hair long like Chayton to respect his Native American lineage, *Ahte's* brown hair scraped the top of his collar in a shaggy way that gave him a sense of wildness.

Desmond, you need to grow it out and braid it, his mother always said in her lilting accent. *I think you're going to shift and run off when you look scraggy like that.*

She'd liked it, though, and Chayton suspected that was why his father didn't change it.

Mato cut straight to the point as soon as they were settled. "You know you don't need to be here."

"Orders," Chayton acknowledged. "But it's a good place for us to mount a search for the rogues."

Mato narrowed his eyes. "They'd die if they stepped foot in city limits."

Typical Mato. Except not all of the colony lived in city limits and no matter how ferocious a shifter was, four to one were not ideal odds. "Which is why we can concentrate on hunting them instead of worrying about the colony's safety."

Mato raised his chin in grudging acknowledgement. Good, Chayton had approached it the right way.

"Has anyone reported any suspicions that the rogues have been sniffing around?" Kaitlyn's tone was respectful and aimed at Mato. She basically ignored his father as if she sensed it'd insult the leader.

Mato shot his gaze toward Kaitlyn like he hadn't expected her to say anything. Chayton sort of wished she'd kept her mouth shut and flown under Mato's radar, but she didn't need coddling. Her quiet confidence and restraint contradicted the redhead with the wild side he'd first met.

"No." From his succinct answer, it looked like Mato would rather swallow napalm than answer her.

Territorial instincts flared in Chayton. He didn't like Mato's condescending gaze on her, nor did he like the attitude wafting off the male. *Ahte's* gaze sharpened on him, but he kept his attention secured on Mato and ignored his father. "Kaitlyn will unload our gear and search the area."

A sneer crossed Mato's face. "You two think you can take on four rogues, but are concerned my whole colony cannot?"

"It's our job." Chayton didn't want things to get ugly, but they would if Mato stood in his way. The rogues had killed and seriously injured mature shifters, accosted females, posed a threat to the young. It was only a matter of time before they turned fully feral and showed no restraint on who and how often they attacked.

"Our initial goal," Kaitlyn interjected before Chayton could argue, "is to prevent them from even getting this far. They don't know we're here. Instead of sneaking up behind them, like we'd be doing if we stayed at Valley Moon, we'll have many more avenues of engagement."

Kaitlyn's steady stare held Mato's incensed one. He was assessing her, deciding if she was worth listening to. Chayton had seen him do it to anyone new to the colony for decades.

Mato leaned back in his chair, his gaze hooked on Kaitlyn's. "You plan to kill them, then?"

She dipped her head in acknowledgement.

Chayton elaborated. "We have a new government, but our methods have not changed. Death is most often the answer. Guardians are entrusted to determine when it's appropriate."

Mato's gaze narrowed on Kaitlyn. "How long have you been a Guardian?"

"Less than ten years."

Chayton almost chuckled. Phrased so she didn't give off the scent of a lie. If she'd been a Guardian even three years yet, he'd be surprised. As far as he knew, she'd only been part of the West Creek Guardians a couple of years before he joined.

"So no bleeding-heart parties for these rogues that terrorize other colonies?" Mato's insinuation that they posed no threat to his colony did not go unnoticed by Chayton.

"The answer was no even before what I saw yesterday." Kaitlyn's vitals remained constant.

Mato didn't intimidate her. Chayton had assumed that her usual partner, Jace, and his ice-blue glare paved the way for her to work among alpha males and females. But she was obviously used to holding her own and didn't fear a physical confrontation.

Finally, Mato pulled his attention off Kaitlyn. "If you're working out of my colony, I want updates. Regularly."

"Of course." Chayton's hackles raised. If Commander Fitzsimmons had said that, he would've been fine. The demand coming from Mato rubbed him raw. Chayton was no longer under Mato's command. Not even when he mated Tika would he be.

Chayton's stomach soured at the reminder of Tika. He could lean over and vomit on the hardwood, but he'd hardly eaten.

Des stood first, as if he had no more interest in the proceedings, and likely he didn't. "Meet me at the house, Chay." His hard gaze swung to Kaitlyn and his eyes softened. "Both of you." He ambled out and was heard murmuring to Zitkana before the front door opened and shut.

Mato's jaw ground at the lack of deference. "You two may go. Notify me when you head into the woods." His eyes pinned on Kaitlyn when he said to Chayton, "I'll let Tika know you're here."

"Appreciate it." Chayton winced at the tendril of a lie that snaked off of him. He spun to exit, sensing Kaitlyn on his heels.

He didn't look forward to Kaitlyn's questions. Not when Mato went out of his way to mention Tika. How could Kaitlyn have made him suspicious in such a short time? Chayton had ensured none of his feelings toward his partner were expressed enough to be sensed.

They both climbed into the vehicle and Kaitlyn cast him a wry look. "Well, he seems pleasant."

Chapter Five

W hy stark relief streaked across Chayton's expression, Kaitlyn couldn't guess. His startled laugh spurred her own.

"That was intense, right?" Chayton's grin ignited a slow burn in her belly.

He pulled away from the house to drive slowly through town. There wasn't much traffic, but like most shifter colonies, they made their actions count and didn't waste time running errands.

His smile died. "When we go hunt, we'll hike into the woods and hide our gear. We shift and search, but we leave town the way we came."

The shifting thing again? "Ashamed?"

Chayton abruptly pulled to the side of the road. He twisted in his seat to face her, his dark eyes deadly serious. "Any weakness will get exploited here, Kaitlyn. You think I'm a dick, wait until you meet every other shifter in this colony. This isn't a place touched by modern inclusive thinking. Their motto is still 'the strong survive,' and if anyone finds out a Guardian roams their streets to enforce how someone else says they should be governed and she can't shift normally, they will use your shifting defect as an example. Mato wouldn't allow anything less."

Chayton's words didn't settle well. Facing Mato without batting an eye had taxed Kaitlyn's mental resources. It was like he had screamed "leave" in her head as soon as she'd sat down in that room. "Does the TriSpecies Synod know about them? It's like a rogue colony, you know."

"Why do you think I was stationed with your pack? The West Creek Guardians police this area and they thought I'd be a good first attempt at mediating things between my home and their government." He paused, a muscle ticking in his jaw. "Besides, it's not the colony, but their leader. Mato's old school."

He abruptly returned to the steering wheel and threw the SUV into gear. Kaitlyn settled back to think on what he said. The village scrolled by, beauty radiating from every facet. Nature was built into each structure, because that was part of shifter DNA. Spirit Moon was no different, but unlike the cottonwoods she was used to, the towering pines lent a regal air to the surroundings.

None of it helped the sense of foreboding that had grown in Kaitlyn's gut during their quick meeting with the posturing leader. The threat of restrictions put on them by Mato compounded the danger of hunting four rogues. She relished the idea of sailing through the trees into guaranteed fighting and injury rather than crossing paths with Mato again.

A dull ached pounded at her temples. When she'd spoken during the meeting, she'd had the urge to shut the fuck up. She was never one to be muscled around, an imaginary voice in her head wasn't going to be the boss of her.

Her normal partner had the power of influence. Jace's pale, intense eyes could persuade anyone to do anything. Did Mato have that power? No, otherwise she would've obeyed. It was probably her nerves after a night of receiving the most powerful pleasure she'd ever known and then getting personally insulted by the giver.

"What?" Chayton asked.

He sensed her inner turmoil. Damn those nerves.

"Nothing."

He might think her shifting issue was a detriment, but he was her real weakness. Emotional struggles could get her killed quicker.

"It's not nothing. You were a cool cucumber going into that place, even after last night…" He cleared his throat and shifted in his seat, as if the memory pierced him with desire like it did her. "We leave and you're fogging the cab with a sense like you're in pain."

"I have a headache. It's nothing. It'll go away." She didn't need to give him another reason to doubt her abilities.

He cut a sharp look toward her. His eyes narrowed, then he swung his gaze back to the road to maneuver a turn that led them deep into the trees. "Mato can be like that."

She suspected Mato could be like a lot of things, but she didn't know what Chayton meant. "Like what, Eagle?"

"I heard his power is like Jace's," Chayton said, snorting, "but not as strong."

So Mato had attempted to force her will. For once Kaitlyn agreed with Chayton's derision. Her pseudo-brother's power of influence couldn't be rivaled. "I felt like Mato would rather I didn't talk."

"You're probably right, but if he had commanded it, you would've obeyed. I've never been on the receiving end—he wouldn't dare—but he didn't gain his position with his personality."

"Why hasn't he used it on you?"

"Because I can use it back on him. I'm sure you've heard the rhyme 'I'm rubber and you're glue, what bounces off of me sticks to you.'"

Kaitlyn stared at him. She'd barely noticed they had pulled into a long driveway that ended in front of small log home. "I can totally see you taunting the rogues with that. Those words are so you. So you're, like, resistant?"

He rolled his eyes at her, but she caught a glimpse of the grin he tried to hide. "No, but I can borrow a power, so to speak, if it's used on me. The effect doesn't last long. I can also harvest another's ability for a short time as long as I know what it is." He stopped under a homemade carport and shut the engine off. "Too bad you don't know what you can do. It'd really help us out with this hunt."

She heard the underlying insinuation: you know, because you faint. "This is your dad's place, huh?"

"Yes, Cinnamon. This hovel is my family's."

She scowled at him. "You know, I wasn't being a bitch. It's surprisingly small, but Des is obviously an ancient and happier in the wild."

"It's relatively new. After *Ahte* settled with my mother, they lived like her people, preferring tepees." Chayton's expression grew solemn. "It was how I grew up. This house wasn't built until after the fire that claimed *Ina*—my mother—and our tepee. Mato demanded a house that blended in with wood or brick."

Chayton got out of the SUV and slammed the door behind him. She marveled over the way he spoke of Mato, his telling displeasure of the colony leader, yet Chayton deferred and respected the male in a way Kaitlyn would never experience from her fellow Guardian. But then she still held affection for a man who'd killed his own wife—her mother—and then himself. Just like her relationship with Chayton, or lack of one, some things weren't black and white.

She climbed out and followed Chayton to the house. He'd grabbed no gear, so she didn't either. Instead of going through the back door, he followed a patio rock path around the back where Des sat in a rocking chair, facing his forested backyard.

The air was still and crisp, filled with the sounds of chirping birds. A sense of peace descended over her. Her short experience with Des was that he wasn't a male whose emotions ran amok and it showed in his quiet, ordered environment. She expected lingering sadness, since he'd lost a mate, but it seemed he'd accepted his lot in life. She always heard when a shifter lost a mate, they sometimes keep living for the children. Perhaps it was that way for Des. Or maybe ancients were different altogether.

She hoped it was the latter. If Des waited for his son to settle down and make babies, it wasn't happening with her.

A feeling of loss almost stalled her, but she shook it off. Kaitlyn hadn't been interested in the tidy mate bond before Chayton swaggered into her life. She'd do fine when he sauntered out. It's not like he could reject her any more than he had.

Des didn't glance at them. His chair rocked rhythmically, his eerie brown eyes straight ahead. Father and son resemblance wasn't so much in looks as in expressions and body language. She would have guessed Chayton's father to have remained in the lifestyle of his deceased mate, but after meeting him, she wondered if he ever had. Or was the Sioux way of life something only Chay and his mother shared.

"*Cinks*," Des's low voice murmured in greeting. He stood and turned to them with a grim expression lacing his welcome.

My son, Chayton filled in for her mentally.

"*Ahte*." Chayton laid a hand on his father's shoulder. Des bowed his head.

Huh. Kaitlyn marveled. She found the one person Chayton showed no hostility to.

Chayton lowered his arm. "We need to unload and get to work."

Des's gaze landed on her. She couldn't escape the sensation like fingers rifling through her mind. She imagined putting a lid on her head as if it was a cookie jar and the feeling went away.

A tiny smirk caught the corner of the ancient's mouth. "Miss Savoy, it's a pleasure."

Chayton's brows drew down and he glanced back and forth between her and his dad. "Have you sensed any danger to the colony, *Ahte*?"

"Not from outside its borders." Slowly, Des pulled his eyes off Kaitlyn, but she caught the satisfied gleam they held. "There is fresh fish in the cooler. Eat before you go."

"We can catch food on the way."

Kaitlyn's stomach heaved. Her genetics said she was a shifter, but the taste center in her brain claimed human. She didn't want to sink her teeth into her meal while its heart still beat. Call her crazy, but she also liked produce and grains and hadn't fully adopted the bacon and milk diet her pack adored.

As if sensing her unease, Des tilted his head toward her. "Fish, yes? I'd like a few minutes to talk before you both take off." Without an answer from them, Des opened the sliding glass door and stepped into the house.

Chayton growled in frustration, but followed. "If you cook, *Ahte*, we'll get settled. I'll take the couch and Kaitlyn can take the spare room if we need to spend any nights in town."

Des slanted a brow at Chayton. "Are you sure staying under my roof wouldn't disappoint T— "

"This is official business."

Kaitlyn raised her own brow at Chayton's interruption. His father gave him an assessing gaze that slid slowly to her. Des wasn't a chatterbox, but he spoke volumes in his expressions. She wished she understood, because she felt like she missed some important facts that the other two knew.

"Very well. They'll be ready if you need to come back and stay." Des busied himself with a frying pan and a tray of white fillets. Chayton spun to step around her and back outside, she turned to follow.

Des spoke quietly. "Miss Savoy?" She stopped and waited for his question. "Who are your parents?"

She heard Chayton's footsteps halt. He threw a warning look over his shoulder, but she dismissed it. Just because he was ashamed of her heritage didn't mean she was. Her cheating mother, homicidal father, and unknown sperm donor birth father were hers to claim.

"My mother was human and she's passed. I don't know who my birth father is."

Des's head jerked toward her. "You weren't raised with him?"

Chayton's tension vibrated across the back deck. If she could flip him the bird without his dad seeing she would. She'd stroll through town announcing her business, and fuck him if he had a problem.

"Nope," she answered, proud that no shame rang through her voice.

Des nodded once. "Interesting. Thank you for answering honestly, Miss Savoy."

Huh. She'd expected the ancient to be part wild, snarling his words as he chewed on a cow femur. Caught in her own stereotyping trap. Instead, Des was civil, articulate, and…passive.

As she strode out past Chayton, who half-glared at her in frustration, she wondered if the ancients that survived the extinction were innately calmer. Perhaps all the ones who'd been wiped out in the mass slaughter were the ones who let instinct rule every action before thought could form. They'd rushed into the fray during the mass targeting of shifters by human hunters and were killed.

She opened the SUV doors and snagged her duffel and rifle bag. When she turned, Chayton stood feet away, arms folded, staring at her. Stepping to the side to let him in to grab his stuff, she kicked her chin up.

They said nothing and she tried not to look at his firm backside sticking out of the door. Her anger at him had dissipated, and she didn't forget the smell of a lie when he'd insulted her. For some reason, he was determined to keep her at a distance.

He straightened with his gear. She raised her attention off his flexing thigh muscles and broad shoulders.

For a second, she saw him with his guard lowered. Astounding depth and emotion that encompassed severe resolve and massive regret was replaced by his usual condescending hint of a sneer. "Let's go inside and eat your *cooked* food."

Yep. That's how it was. Only the longer she was around him, the more she saw that his words reinforced his walls, but didn't represent his true feelings.

Still, she deserved better.

***

She deserved better.

Chayton organized his gear for the fifth time. It wasn't like he could take much of it with him if they were going to stow it in a hiding spot and search as wolves. The busywork helped him sort through the conflict raging within him.

His dad liked Kaitlyn. Mato hated her. Tika might drop by anytime. Chayton's fierce need to protect Kaitlyn gave way to admiration of her diplomatic and field skills. He no longer scorned her inability to shift back to being a human without blacking out, but his concern over it harming her had grown exponentially.

Ahte hadn't batted an eye at Kaitlyn's humanness admission, but Chayton often forgot his *ina* was human. His father had indulged every last one of *Ina's* wishes to retain as much of her tribe as he could. But since she had been gone, Chayton witnessed his father's true mellow nature. His *ahte* was genial, but not friendly, yet Kaitlyn had almost gotten a smile out of him in the first minute after they'd arrived.

Had his dad figured out the redhead was Chayton's mate? Was that why he'd tried to mention Tika, to test it? Des hadn't been involved in Chayton's promise to Tika, but then he'd been reeling over *Ina's* death.

Chayton rubbed his face. Mato's insistence that Chayton mate his daughter began shortly after the girl was born. Then *Ina* died in that horrible fire and Chayton had thought discussions were tabled, but Zitkana had come back at him full force. Like promising himself to Tika decades before she could have a say could erase his overwhelming grief at the loss of his mother.

His stomach growled at the delicious smells originating in the kitchen. He hoped *Ahte* fried up at least twenty fish. Unlike Kaitlyn, he wasn't averse to eating on the run, but it'd take time and could alert the rogues to their presence.

Kaitlyn exited the tiny guest room and padded to the kitchen. She had some balls. His dad intimidated most shifters with his intense scrutiny and here she was seeking him out.

Their voices drifted to him. Her laugh made Chayton think of meadowlarks on a sunny day.

He got up and stomped to the kitchen to see Kaitlyn setting the round table that'd barely fit the three of them.

"I think your cooking will be just fine, Des." A smile lingered on her stunning face. "You'll have to tell me about the fishing holes around here."

Chayton's eyes widened. Not only was she chatting up his dad, but she was subtly collecting information about her surroundings.

A grin, an actual grin, stretched his dad's face, delight dancing in his brown eyes. "These fish came from a lake I feared no longer held fish once Chayton started swimming in it as a boy. Every time he went for a swim, he came home with no less than ten fish. Always *hokuwa*."

Always fishing. His *ina* had chided him each time. *Cinks, you must learn about balance.*

Chayton smiled unbidden at that memory. His memories concentrated on his mother's fierceness, but she'd been warm and loving, too.

The back of his throat clogged. He cleared it. "Thanks for cooking."

His father nodded in his always-knowing way. Chayton wondered if *Ahte's* sense of loss rose in a tidal wave whenever he visited.

Kaitlyn's smile faltered. "Can I get anything else for the table?"

Des frowned and scanned the plain, cozy kitchen. "Am I missing something?"

"No," Chayton answered. "She likes to eat what grows out of the ground, not just what roams the earth."

Understanding dawned on Des's face. "Yes. Nita loved to gather. Never got a taste for leaves, myself."

Chayton rested his hands on top of his chair at the table and hoped it didn't get awkward. Kaitlyn would guess the Nita mentioned was his mother.

"Don't worry about me. I don't complain about people feeding me." Kaitlyn waited by her chair until Chayton's father approached the table.

Ahte rested the sizzling cast iron pan on the table trivet and dished a heaping portion out to each of them.

"Sit, sit." *Ahte* waved at them before he settled onto his chair. "I'm too old to dwell on ceremony."

They devoured their food in silence. As forks scraped plates, his father calmly studied his guests.

"What path will you take to hunt for the beasts?" *Ahte* hated including rogues and ferals among shifterkind. In his opinion, they weren't worthy of being a human or a wolf.

Chayton tended to agree. "The deer trail that loops around Four Waters. We can use the lakes to mask our scent, and if the rogues know the area, they'd do the same if they planned to attack the colony."

Ahte nodded in approval. He'd probably come up with the same plan and tested Chayton with it.

"Is Four Waters one lake or four?" Kaitlyn asked.

Ahte slid his dishes to the side and used his fingers to draw an imaginary map. "My plate is the cabin. The trail circles around each of the four lakes. They're separate bodies of water, but are situated like a four-leaf clover."

"Maybe they'll be lucky like one." Kaitlyn rose and collected the plates.

Ahte didn't look at her when he asked, "How long have you really been a Guardian, Miss Savoy?"

Her hands stilled arranging the dishes in the sink, one hand clenched around a dish rag. "Almost three years."

Ahte chuckled, his dark eyes crinkling at the corners. "Most definitely under ten years. You are not in tune with your wolf, but you're a Guardian?"

Chayton's eyes widened. He caught Kaitlyn's accusatory look and shook his head.

His father stood. "*Cinks* said nothing, but I'm grateful he knows. That kind of disconnect endangers you both. How does it express itself?"

Her mouth opened, but nothing came out. It snapped shut and she clenched her jaw. Humiliation and anger rolled off her in waves.

"I don't blame you for not wanting to talk about it, but I suggest you put the pieces in your psyche back together before it gets you killed." *Ahte* stepped through the sliding door, shed his clothing, transformed.

Chayton had seen it a million times, but a startled gasp escaped Kaitlyn as the massive, shaggy creature that resembled a humanoid wolf loped off on two legs. She'd only seen Cian from a distance yesterday; his father must be her first experience with an ancient shifting.

"He's right," Chayton murmured.

"No shit." Kaitlyn slapped the dishcloth down and stormed to her room.

Chayton pinched the bridge of his nose. That could've gone better.

A knock sounded on the door. Who'd come calling on his father? *Ahte* defined the term loner.

With a sigh, he pushed himself up and made his way to the front door. He glanced out to see a little red coupe parked behind the SUV.

Fuuuck. Did this have to happen now? An ominous feeling descended, like the Grim Reaper waited on the other side rather than the young female he wished had stayed in town. His future mate.

He swung open the front door. "Tika."

The sultry brunette smiled wide and pulled him down for a kiss. Her warm lips touched his and he refrained from pushing her back at the wrongness of the feeling. As soon as her pink tongue swept across his mouth, he pulled away.

"I'm sorry, Tika. I'm working. Can we talk later?"

Her smiled faltered, and her gentle forest-green eyes grew concerned. "Chay, you've been away so long, I hoped we could reconnect. It's not like you haven't stopped through while you're working before."

A sexy pout curved her mouth. It was then he noticed her flowy skirt and light sweater. He called it easy access clothing. His manhood remained silent. Sure, last year he'd been more than tempted by the tasty little morsel in front of him. Tika's native looks, exotic eyes, and strong, curvy body enticed any male she came across. Chayton's agreement to bond with her might've been made based on logistics alone, but his time spent in her arms during his last visit had supported his decision all those years ago.

Only now he wondered what the fuck he'd gotten himself into. His body had screamed for release for the last several weeks only to shut down when facing his future mate because she wasn't the redhead destined for him.

Destiny was a cold bitch. Almost twenty-five years he'd been sworn to someone else and fate drops his true mate on him months before he was to bond with Tika.

"I'm on a case and I need to leave for a hunt."

Her voice dropped to a husky purr. "You can't even spare five minutes?"

Sweet Mother. His promised mate wanted a quick fuck while his destined mate was in the other room. This painted him all shades of slimy idiot.

"We're literally ready to step out the door. I'll call you when we get back."

Her expression filled with regret. "No problem. Father will let me know when you return. Then you and I get some time together. We need to set a date."

He forced a charming smile. "Deal."

She sauntered away, her hips swaying and lifting the skirt to reveal creamy cinnamon thighs.

It wasn't the cinnamon he wanted to lick. Lust roared into him, hot and hard.

He shut the front door and listened to the car drive away. His chest heaved; desire swamped him. Tika left and any emotion he should've felt for her swamped him.

Why now?

Because he'd thought of cinnamon.

"I thought I heard someone at the door?" Kaitlyn's head popped out of her room. She sniffed and raised a brow. "An admirer."

Her sardonic expression faded when Chayton swung his head toward her. She straightened, almost disappearing behind the door jam. "Eagle, you all right?"

The roiling turmoil inside of him focused on the maddening, damaged Guardian. He was moving before he realized it, unhooking his shoulder holster and dropping it in the hallway. By the time he curved into the bedroom, his weapon belt had hit the floor.

Kaitlyn's mouth opened, her eyes filled with understanding, but she didn't back away.

Out of the corner of his vision, he saw her gear spread out over the bed. She must've been checking and loading everything for the hunt. Like him, she was just in her leathers and her shirt.

Her pink tongue flicked out to lick her lips—it hadn't even touched him and the sight hit him like a grizzly bear. He wanted it on him. His body wanted to wipe out the feeling of the other female's tongue.

Oh, no. He'd taste like Tika if Kaitlyn kissed him.

The room was tiny enough. It took only two steps to back Kaitlyn against the wall. She drew in a breath, her pupils expanded. "Eagle?"

Last time, in her passion she called him Chay. Would she do it again?

"I want to see if you taste like spice." He didn't recognize the gruff, guttural voice that came from his mouth.

He dropped to his knees and yanked at the clasp on her pants.

Her head dropped back to hit the wall. "Don't think this will make me forgive you."

"I'm not looking for forgiveness." He wanted to forget—about the rogues, about Tika, about his stupid promise, about honor. He just wanted to consume Kaitlyn.

As his hands worked around her waistband to draw her pants down around her hips, she stepped out of her boots.

The scent of her hit as soon as her pants cleared her lushly rounded ass. She wanted him. He dragged her pants down, and as soon as she kicked them out of the way, he lifted a leg. Her womanhood on display in front of him.

His fangs throbbed. "You're glistening for me and I haven't even touched you."

"You seem to have that effect on me." Her breathless words sent more blood streaming to his shaft. His own pants were painfully tight, but he wasn't going to do anything about it. Not yet. Not until he made her scream his name first.

Her calf rested across his shoulder. He used his fingers to separate her and lick her from her opening to the bundle of nerves waiting for his touch.

She cried out. Her hips bucked against him. "Do it again."

Yesss, she was as desperate for him as he was for her. Rational thought threatened to invade and it had no place in this moment. Nothing was stopping him.

He lapped at her. She writhed, her hands fisted in his hair. She demanded more, faster. He licked and nibbled. Wet, so wet. It was all his. The previous night he'd gotten an appetizer, but this was decadent dessert. After he finished consuming her, he'd go for the main meal.

She was close to exploding, riding his face. He used one hand to crank her leg up and his other to insert a finger. Her sex clenched around him. She moaned his name, encouragement, then her words jumbled together because he withdrew and thrust in a second finger.

He felt her climax whip through her. She released against his face and he lapped up every last drop, using his fingers to wring each second of pleasure. He would've stayed, coaxed her to another peak, but his body demanded more.

A button popped off and clattered across the hardwood. He shoved and tugged at the material, the haze of need blinding him until cool air breezed across his shaft.

Kissing his way up Kaitlyn's body, he suspected he was the only thing holding her up. Her leg had fallen limp, her foot hitting the floor with a thud.

She snatched his shirt over his head and he did the same to hers. Her breasts needed to be pressed against him. A growl surfaced at the sports bra she wore. Too impatient to remove it, he yanked it down until her nipples were free.

Pausing only to suck one into his mouth and palm the other, his manhood jerked, warning him that it'd release on its own this close to the object of its obsession.

Chayton rose to stand over her and gaze deep into her lovely emerald eyes. The color soothed his soul—the right shade on the right female. He gripped her thighs and wrapped her legs around his waist and impaled her in one thrust.

Kaitlyn's eyes flew wide open with her gasp. She settled onto him, adjusting to his size.

"You don't know how long I've been waiting for that." Her hands were back in his hair, tugging his head down to her lips.

He set the most natural rhythm in the world. She matched. His hips worked in and out. He would've exploded already, but he feared to never feel this good again. Their mouths connected, their sex connected. The strongest urge to kiss his way down her neck and mark her swept through him. He fought it. No. No claiming today. Just sex. Mind-blowing sex.

Her legs hugged his waist so tight, he could barely thrust. Rocking into her wet heat was enough. Ripples traveled through her and along his shaft. The first wave of climax.

Kaitlyn ripped her face away from his to throw her head to the side, unconsciously baring herself for him. Chayton's fangs throbbed, his eyes locked onto her neck, centuries of species instinct rammed at his skull to mark her, to tell every male she crossed that she belonged to someone: him.

Her walls fisted him. She panted and gasped, then the full impact of orgasm hit her and almost knocked Chayton back. The power of her pleasure pushed him past his own crest.

"Chay!" she cried. Her fingernails tore into his shoulders as she bucked and writhed.

He pumped his release into her, his fingers digging into her thighs, and when he glanced down, the sight of her round breasts fueled the strength of his climax.

Her neck—it was right there. Throwing his head back, he growled out all the frustration eating at him until he roared her name.

They both fell quiet as his hips gently rocked them down from their atmospheric heights. Rational thought finally knocked on his brain.

What the fuck did he just do?

"No," Kaitlyn murmured. She sighed and turned up her face to meet his gaze. "Don't just drop me and storm out."

The way his hands gripped the smooth skin of her thighs, he didn't know if he could coax them into giving Kaitlyn up. At least not now, after she spoke. Because he had been ready to dump and run to figure this mess out away from the siren call of her body.

He gently lifted her off him and steadied her until her feet were once more firmly on the ground.

"This can't happen." It was all he could say, as if that explanation would make it better when he left her to mate with Tika. Kaitlyn had to feel the link between them, the deep attraction, near obsession that flagged a mate, even if her human upbringing didn't allow her to understand what it meant.

Hurt flashed across her face, but she covered it quickly. Not before it stabbed him in the heart. He was such a bastard.

She pushed her fingertips against his chest. "We have a job to do. Let's just worry about that first."

Her little touch and his shaft was full and ready to go. She had already turned away to gather clothing. Her lithe, nude body…blood pounded though him. His desire didn't just fill the room, but the whole cabin. His father was going to choke on it when he got back.

Chayton eyed the spread of weapons on the bed as he stuffed his throbbing manhood into his pants. "Pack everything in a bag. After our shift, we can carry it with us."

"Won't that slow us down?"

"Yes, but if we can use firepower to take out one or two before a physical confrontation, it'll be best."

She shrugged into her black top, not looking at him. "You're worried I'll zone out again."

"It's a possibility." He half-turned and forced himself not to watch her, or he'd have her up against the wall again in seconds. "Look, I'm not saying you and I can't take on four and win. I'd bet on us. But there's more than our ego at risk and we need to ensure we take out the threat."

"Why don't we shift now and head out?" She appeared as if nothing was wrong, but the forceful shoving of weapons into the duffel suggested otherwise.

"In case we need to shift back within city limits."

She shook her head, her jaw rigid, tension radiating from her. He wondered if she was mad at him, or herself.

Chapter Six

Something was up with that big lunk. No way was he telling her.

And who was the female that she heard talking? Was she what got Chayton all riled up? Should Kaitlyn thank her or hate her?

Because that was the best sex she'd ever imagined. And it was with just one guy. No wonder all the mated couples in her pack hit it with each other whenever possible. Kaitlyn thought it was because shifters have strong sexual appetites and once mated, they didn't have to go searching for a partner or two to try to satisfy it.

No clue that mate sex was so much better than unbonded sex. Except he'd made it clear less than a minute after orgasm that it'd only be unbonded-mate-sex.

Asshole.

Yet she'd been an open door for him to enter.

Anger with herself rose another notch. Like she didn't have a bad enough track record with men, or no record worth noting. She was forgettable. Except to Waylon, a good friend and a male who didn't insult her.

When Chayton walked away for good, at least she had the bartender until he found his own mate.

Yes, she'd let Chayton walk away. Mate or not, she respected the hell out of herself, despite what her easy acquiescence earlier showed. There'd be no begging, she wouldn't cry for him to be with her. Destiny could go off itself if she had to settle for a mate who treated her badly and didn't want her. Wouldn't happen.

She zipped her duffle shut, blanked her expression, and walked outside where Chayton waited. The heft of her bag shouldn't be a problem as a wolf, but it'd be a nuisance. Still, cold metal in her hand was more natural than fangs and claws and she'd be glad to have her guns.

Without a word, Chayton hiked into the trees. His own worn leather satchel was much smaller— her sniper skills meant she carried bigger guns. With acute wolf senses, her ability to hit long-range shots proved an advantage.

For any other reason, a day in the forest would be nice. But they'd be running as much as the terrain allowed. The bite in the air would keep them from overheating. Evening approached, meaning they'd either travel at night, or hunker down. It'd be Chayton's choice. Kaitlyn had slept in worse places while on duty.

They traversed a few miles in silence when Chayton pulled behind a tree. His eyes squinted into the landscape. She followed his lead and inhaled deep. The faint scent of two shifters tickled her nose, along with a smell of meat that'd make her stomach growl if she wasn't still full of fish.

The males trotted away from them, their dusky coats easily blending into the floor of the forest.

She exchanged a look with Chayton and they both went to investigate, moving slowly even though the shifters were out of sight. Stealth prevented their smell from aerating through the trees and kept any noise down.

"You smell that right?" Chayton mumbled.

Kaitlyn rolled her eyes at him. They stopped and stared at a small heap at the base of a tree. The ground had been dug into and surrounding brush had been laid over it. If any more time had lapsed, the cover would've smothered the scent of what it hid.

He shrugged. "Just checking. Find a stick to probe with. I don't want us covered with meat juice while we're hunting."

While he squatted and inspected the surrounding areas, she retrieved a two-foot long stick. On the opposite side of the pile, Kaitlyn knelt and pushed aside some of the concealment.

"Steaks?" Chayton ducked his head to get a look at the entire hiding spot. "Is someone hoarding food or what?"

"Or leaving it for someone—or something. Maybe they're feeding a bear." His sardonic expression irritated her. "As if you haven't experienced weirder shit than that. Last year, Jace and I had to deal with a family who killed a mama bear to adopt her cubs."

"I don't see anyone from my colony adopting a bear."

"Do you see them leaving enough steaks out here to feed several shifters?" Her question was meant to be sarcastic, but her eyes widened.

Chayton's gaze narrowed on the steaks. "Like four shifters?"

"Why would they feed the rogues? I haven't caught their scent yet." But the idea certainly made sense. "Although…we don't know what colony they came from. Usually, the Guardians are notified because the rogues may pose a threat to their original colony, or will eventually once they turn feral."

"Except Mato sees it as a sign of power and competency to deal with everything himself." Chayton huffed and rolled his eyes skyward as if his frustration with the leader reached new heights. "Cover it back up. They might not smell us if they don't get here right away. *If* it's intended for the rogues."

"We limit our search to a radius around this food, then?"

He nodded grimly. Maybe they were wrong. But neither of them thought so.

***

They were well into nighttime. They'd covered a good swath of the area, but had detected nothing.

Kaitlyn's flanks heaved with the effort. The farther out they got, the rougher the terrain—steep inclines and at times, too rapid of a descent. Her side still ached, not yet mended from the tumble down the side of a nearly sheer drop.

One more mile and we're back to our campsite. Chayton sounded like he looked, which was no more troubled than if he'd been taking an easy jog on a flat bike path.

He'd run this land for years and years, she reminded herself. The forest was different from the woods.

At least earlier she'd caught that enormous rodent on the first try. Chayton had told her it was a *sikpela*, but she'd ripped into it and devoured her share without really taking a look. She seriously hated when her food stared back at her.

Minutes later, she spotted, with relief, the incline that harbored an overhang on the other side. Under that minuscule amount of shelter was where they'd camp. Easing up the embankment and leaping to the ground on the other side, she dropped her bag and flexed her jaw.

Chayton trotted around to face her. He flowed into his mouth-watering human form. *Now you need to shift back.*

She would've wanted to lick her lips, but his words doused her with cold water. *Why? Aren't we going to sleep like this?*

Are you going to magically wait for a cure to your problem? You know why you pass out, now push through it.

The image of her dad looming over her with his shotgun, the smell of her mom's blood, increased the pressure behind her eyes. She shook her head like she was shaking off water droplets.

Chayton had a good point. This hang-up haunted her wherever she went. They always planned around it. With Jace, it was second nature, and he never mentioned it. Commander Fitzsimmons avoided sending her anywhere that didn't utilize her shooting abilities, her democratic nature, or her hand-to-hand skills. As long as the op didn't require her to get furry.

She had to deal with it.

Okay. She closed her eyes and concentrated on her human form, imagined it, embraced the shift. Blackness encroached. She fought to stay present, fought to keep her wits with her.

Darkness won.

Kaitlyn blinked her eyes open. She was lying in the dirt under the outcropping where they'd set up camp. The outline of a long-haired male stood over her, moonlight casting shadows on his features.

"Get up and try it again." Chayton didn't offer a hand up.

She scowled at him and rose on her own, shrugging off any remaining wooziness. Night life was slowly coming alive, but the sound seemed muted. She shifted back to her wolf before she told Chayton she couldn't.

She gazed up at his dark, unreadable eyes and caught a slight scent of worry. Not what she expected from the way he scorned her deficiency.

"Again." His flat tone matched his stare.

This time she kept her eyes open. She picked a tree and focused on her transition. A tremor wracked her body with her effort to remain conscious.

Fuzziness began at the periphery of her vision.

No, no, no. She wouldn't pass out. Fur gave way…

Darkness.

Déjà vu. She groggily gazed up at Chayton.

"Get up and try again." His voice thudded between her ears.

She groaned and rolled to her side to get up.

"How long was I out?" She held her head as she rose. One killer headache started to build.

"A couple minutes."

The hint of worry from him had grown. "Like two minutes or, I don't know, it seemed like longer but was probably only two minutes?"

"Does it matter?"

Yeah, actually. The way her head felt, she wanted to know if she was going to knock herself out for an hour with this experiment.

She huffed her exasperation and shifted back to her wolf. The headache stayed with the shift.

This time, she waited longer before she attempted her human form.

"Again." Chayton pulled her up.

She swayed when she hit her feet. Chayton's strong grip steadied her.

"Five times is enough," she slurred. Holy fucking migraine. She pinched one eye shut and squinted with the other. It was full-on night, but even moonlight overpowered her oculars.

She just wanted to collapse into him, but instead she shifted before she just plain collapsed.

Even as a wolf, she laid on her belly. Burying her nose in the dirt seemed like a good idea. Her stomach rumbled, but the way her head pounded, she'd probably just throw up anything she ate.

Chayton said that damn word again. "Again." Only it was almost a whisper.

His concern fogged the area. How long had she been out last time?

She closed her eyes. Drew in several cleansing breaths. Fully embraced herself as a canine. Sharper smells, every draft of air teased individual fur fibers, sounds she swore were from miles away. Her senses *rocked*. The headache eased slightly.

Time to shift.

She couldn't help the whimper that escaped. Open eyes worked better; she chose a tree to focus on and concentrated.

Fur gave way to skin. Kaitlyn heard the whine and registered it came from her, but she was determined to stay with it.

The pressure in her head increased. An image of her father standing over her branded her vision. The tree her gaze bored into grew smaller and smaller, and the world grew even darker.

Stay. Awake.

She adjusted her legs because suddenly they were stacked. Skin-on-skin.

No urge to rejoice could push past the agony behind her eyes. Her breath came in quick pants until blackness claimed her.

"Kaitlyn." A strong hand shook her shoulder, warm breath blew across her face.

The masculine scent that was imprinted in her psyche wafted by, rousing her. Her mate. She tried to speak, but nothing made it past thought.

"Sweet Mother." He stroked her face, his fingers played over her jawline. His thumb caressed her lower lip. "Kaitlyn. Please wake up."

She registered his lap under her. He cradled her head in one arm as her body draped across his legs. The heat of him staved off most of the chill in the air.

A moan finally escaped. "I hurt."

He blew out a relieved breath. "At least you're finally healing. You were so still and pale for so long."

"How long?" It came out as a croak. She licked her lips, but a dry tongue from cotton mouth wasn't too effective.

"Hours."

Another groan and she curled into him, pulling her legs up to get warm. He changed position stretched out next to her, sandwiching her between him and the wall of stone. She shivered against the coolness of the rock. He clutched her tighter and the wall quickly lost its bite.

"I got further that last time," she mumbled into his chest.

"It cost you." His chin rested on top of her head.

Damn, he felt good. Her body heated up in places she should ignore.

Chayton didn't. "Is this position too much? Are you too warm now?"

"Mmm." She rolled onto her back, using the movement to pull him on top of her. His muscles bunched under her hands to move away, but she held him in place.

"Kaitlyn, I can't…" His argument had to sound weak to even his own ears.

"Make me feel good, Eagle."

His conflicted emotions were apparent in what little moonlight filtered through the pines. The thick band of his arousal throbbed between them. Refusal faded in his gaze when he focused on her mouth. He dropped his head and their lips met.

Fire stormed though her. She was so *hot*. Parting her legs allowed him to sink between them. It didn't make sense that she needed to be closer to him to make the burn feel better, but she didn't care. Her head no longer hurt, the exquisite weight of his body, the dark cove that was theirs alone, and being in her most comfortable form after so many debilitating shifts all combined to fuel this moment.

He started gentle, but she needed more. Her tongue brushed across the seam of his lips and her body responded to his taste. Pressure mounted between her legs and the heat pouring off her created a sheen of sweat across them both.

She bit and nibbled at his lips. Sensing her urgency, he gripped her leg to bring it up to his side and angled his shaft at her entrance.

She moaned and ran her hands down his back to clench his ass. Her reaction encouraged him like she meant it to. He impaled her with a swift thrust.

Breaking contact, she turned her face away to cry, "*Yes.*"

It wasn't an adequate word but it encompassed everything her body called for. Pleasure from the aggravating male who hooked onto her every thought.

He withdrew and slammed into her again. She gasped, but didn't release her grip on his butt. Sultry kisses trailed down her neck, over her collarbone, farther until he latched onto one taut nipple. Her hands skimmed up his back to cradle his head to her.

With his every push, she met him with equal force. Dirt abraded her back, but the chafing released some of the pent-up emotion. God, her unstable emotions, they caused the searing heat, fueled and stoked it. She was so damn *frustrated*, and mad. Angry at herself for passing out after every shift, pissed that she couldn't keep from wanting Chayton, upset with him for making her feel this way but refusing to be with her, his mate.

A growl escaped her, mixed with Chayton's grunts. His teeth clamped at her breast, nothing but delicious pain.

His hips bucked wildly, her climax built with each thrust, her face was still turned away. Raw sex. That's all it was and it was perfect.

She gasped before her orgasm slammed home. Her back bowed, her cry echoed into the night, and she registered Chayton's last push. Her body was finally cooling off even as his hot release spilled inside her.

They shook and trembled together. At some point, his head came to rest between her breasts. They trembled together, heaving for breath.

If there wasn't steam coming off of them, she'd be surprised. She'd look, but her eyelids suddenly weighed at least eighty pounds. Sleep pulled her under just as Chayton rolled them to their sides with her in his embrace.

Chapter Seven

Faint rays of light brightened the early morning sky. Chayton lay on his back with one arm thrown behind his head, his other arm curled around slumbering Kaitlyn.

He hadn't slept at all. How could he after his guilt at forcing her to go through shift after shift transitioned to mind-blowing sex? Their coupling probably lasted all of two minutes. Best two minutes ever spent.

Sweet Mother, how was he supposed to go through bonding with another female after that? Already his memories of being with Tika had faded, but he knew it was like comparing a night on eight-count sheets to eight-hundred-count sheets. Fuck, even that was too narrow of a comparison.

And he was hard again.

No more. If he had sex with Kaitlyn again, he didn't know if he'd be strong enough to refrain from marking her.

Maybe he should tell her. Maybe they could work something out, find a solution. She had the skills to stay alive if Mato sought revenge against her, or just wanted to take out his anger on her instead of Chayton.

What would *Ahte* think? His father wouldn't take breaking an oath lightly, especially one as significant as a blood vow. Then there was Kaitlyn's family history and her bloodlines, or lack of any heritage.

What were his choices? Fail his father, Mato and his daughter, and his whole village, or disappoint Kaitlyn. Once he mated Tika, he'd have to move back home. No more Kaitlyn.

An ache blossomed in his chest.

He gently disengaged from Kaitlyn. She stirred and murmured something before her eyes fluttered open. His gut clenched at the intelligent green eyes that searched for his.

"We need to go." His gruff tone made him sound angry, and he was, dammit. For making a vow only a foolish, immature shifter would make. He hadn't been young by any means, but two centuries had passed without a hint that he'd meet his destined mate. It gave a guy the wrong idea, the impression that he'd be alone for centuries, or worse, grow feral from the lack of a mating bond and become one of the depraved individuals he hunted for a living.

Confusion and hurt flickered in her gaze, but was quickly replaced with a neutral expression. "What's the plan for today?"

He dug through his bag, extracted two protein bars, and tossed one to Kaitlyn. Raw meat was preferred, but taking the time to hunt hindered their search.

She snatched it out of the air and sat up, unashamed of her glorious nudity. His desire had to be obvious, it's why he sat with his back half turned to her.

"I go in wolf form. You take your rifle and follow."

The both chewed their meager breakfast.

"And if I see them?" She tugged her clothes closer to her to sort through them. "Shoot to kill?"

He turned fully away. Starting the day with her in his arms was difficult enough. Watching her dress would be torture. "After what we saw, we have more than enough to execute all four of them."

The sooner the rogues were killed, the sooner he and Kaitlyn went their separate ways.

His stomach roiled. No, his body did not like that thought. Not at all.

"I can pack our gear." Shuffling sounds behind him meant she was dressing.

He steadied his gaze into the trees, not daring to look back until she was clothed head-to-toe. "If you can haul it, we won't have to return." *I won't have to be reminded about the erotic quickie.* As if he'd ever forget. "We can make a wider arc around the colony."

He packed his things. More like shuffled it around because it was already loaded. When he sensed she was completely done, he double-checked that she was ready.

What a beautiful female. Her standard copper braid hung down her back, and black tactical attire accentuated every curve. A long rifle was slung across her back, its shoulder strap resting between her breasts like Chayton had done hours ago.

How could she be so enticingly feminine, yet tough and soldierlike at the same time? It wasn't just his bias because she was his mate.

Every male she swayed those hips past dropped his jaw. Her striking hair alone was enough for that, but the confidence in her stride and her zest for life endeared her to others immediately.

She'd make someone a lucky mate someday.

Rage rose swiftly within him. He flowed into his wolf before it took over and he claimed her there to make a point.

If she sensed his sudden change in mood, she ignored it. He spun out, chunks of dirt flying up behind him. His rage found an outlet in the run. Behind him, he heard Kaitlyn's steady footsteps. Her fitness level would allow her to run for hours, but Chayton set a moderate pace. They'd covered many miles the previous night, and while the rogues could be moving forward, toward them, he wanted to cover a larger radius before dark. It wasn't a fact that the group they searched for targeted Spirit Moon, but something inside Chayton screamed that they would.

Hours passed before Chayton wove his way through the trees to a lake nestled into a natural bowl formation in the terrain. It was the nearest lake of the Four Waters grouping. He ordered Kaitlyn to drink and refuel with an energy bar. He did the same, only his fuel was still kicking when he devoured it.

He and Kaitlyn hadn't said any more between them. As he had ran and scented the environment for hints of the rogues, his concentration continuously faltered and swung toward the sexy redhead. For the thousandth time, he wondered if he shouldn't tell her why he acted the way he did. He'd already alluded to how his colony might treat her and that was correct; look at how he'd reacted to her.

Licking his chops, he scanned their surroundings. Blue water glittered from the sun, offsetting the surrounding green. Its smell was fresher thanks to the lower temps.

Crackles from Kaitlyn's wrapper could barely be heard. She incorporated stealth into everything she did in the field. Had she been like that as a human?

He could ask her.

Nah. Tasting her, being inside of her, made it hard enough to walk away. Getting to know her just hurt them both.

Kaitlyn quenched her thirst after she ate; then it was his turn. He approached the water's edge. Small rocks bit into his feet, but he followed the normal path of wildlife in the area. Cold water sluiced down his throat. He guessed they'd covered ten miles. Not much if they were on the road, but the forest offered several more obstacles.

Distant barks perked his ears. He raised his head, water dripping off his chin. He sensed Kaitlyn finish loading her pack and shrugging it on. Chayton backed slowly away from the water's edge, constantly scanning around him.

More barks filtered through the trees.

They're on our left. Kaitlyn had made it back farther, effectively camouflaging herself. Chayton hadn't reached cover yet when the fur rose on his back. He heard a quick intake of breath from Kaitlyn and his eyes drifted up.

The ridge that bordered the other side of the lake was covered in pines, but Chayton made out four forms between them.

We go after them. He continued backing up.

I have my sights centered. I can take the shot. Her steady answer held no doubt that she wouldn't miss.

From this far away? Chayton forced himself not to look at her in case the rogues hadn't discovered her. *Silver-laced bullets?*

Absolutely.

Take the shot.

The last word left his mind when the blast sounded. It echoed through the trees. One of the four forms whipped backward, his yelp darkly satisfying to Chayton. A mutiny of barks broke out.

He glanced at Kaitlyn. She was on her belly, leg kicked out to the side, rifle to her nose, steadying on another target.

She blew out a breath and hopped up. She slung the rifle back over her shoulder. "Too much movement. I can't get a good sight."

Chayton swung his head back. She was right. They were gone. He concentrated and detected movement. *They're coming this way.*

"Yes." Her hard expression followed the rogues' advance. "Most shifters run the other way after a silver encounter."

They're rogues and they know it's just you and me.

Kaitlyn withdrew a pistol from the waist holster wrapped around her hips. "These bullets haven't been dipped in a silver wash. They won't kill them, but a shot between the eyes slows a shifter the fuck down."

Nice. No wonder Commander Fitzsimmons relied on her shooting skills. Fangs and claws were Chayton's best weapons. He studied their surroundings, this time not for concealment but for confrontation.

If we wait here, they'll know we're waiting for them. Circle around the lake toward them, but no farther than the east edge, before it turns into a dropoff. We can use the trees and the rocks but still have room to fight.

Got it.

Chayton led the way. Frenzied barks echoed all around them. He made out two males and the female. Kaitlyn had killed one of the males. Too bad it was the one who had triggered the flashback and paralyzed her the last time they fought.

Snarls of rage reached him before he saw three forms flowing around tree trunks. Could Kaitlyn hit a moving target while she was also moving?

Her gun blasted behind him. A yelp rang out and the pale wolf jerked sideways but recovered and kept charging.

A hundred more yards and he'd encounter the first shifter. Another blast fired. Bark flew off a tree trunk, but Kaitlyn's shot missed.

Bared teeth and fangs lunged to meet Chayton. Kaitlyn fired another shot. The wolf he was facing flinched and yelped, but his momentum carried forward until he collided with Chayton.

Their teeth smashed against each other. Blood welled in Chayton's mouth, a mix of both of theirs.

Claws ripped down his side with a stream of burning agony from the torn flesh. Chayton whipped his head back and forth until he had a clear path to the rogue's neck. He grabbed the opening and sunk his fangs into the flesh. The rogue thrashed and tried to howl. He and Chayton whipped around in circles as the rogue frantically tried to free himself. Chayton ground his jaws, searching for the jugular to bleed the fucker out.

More gunshots were heard. He raised his eyes as far as he could. Kaitlyn faced off against the other two wolves, who were using the trees for protection.

Kaitlyn feinted right, then left and tricked the female to reveal a flank. Kaitlyn took the shot and the rogue fell to her haunches. The other rogue sent out a commanding howl.

Chayton used his limbs to fend off swipes by the male he held. He opened his mouth wider and bit down harder. Blood streamed into his mouth. Jackpot. Seconds passed and the rogue he held grew weak.

The other two rogues managed to flank Kaitlyn. His mate pulled another gun out and held both out to either side.

Badass.

Chayton needed just a few more seconds before the rogue he grappled with was subdued.

Again, his hackles raised. What the—

He sensed the fourth rogue before he saw the dark shadow jump for Kaitlyn.

Behind you! His jaw dropped, releasing his prey. The rogue collapsed to the ground.

Kaitlyn spun, her arm rose higher to shoot the shifter, but he was too fast. Chayton lunged as Kaitlyn switched to defensive tactics to keep the wolf's jaws away from her too-human, too-fragile throat.

The gun fell to the ground. Kaitlyn was shoved back to the ground with the male on top of her, his claws planted into her belly. She grunted, her blood tinged the air. Her arms were getting ripped to shreds from his fangs, but she kept the male from getting a good purchase on her. Blood bloomed across the shifter's side from Kaitlyn's earlier shot. Why hadn't the silver killed him yet? Had it been just a flesh wound? Couldn't he just lie down and die?

Chayton bared his teeth at the setback. The male Chayton had fought hadn't recovered yet, but the remaining two stalked Chayton. Both were bleeding from gunshot wounds, but not enough to adequately weaken them.

The male's eyes unfocused for a split second. Damn, they were communicating, plotting.

The female darted to the side, the male lunged. Chayton had no choice but to take on the male, but he didn't trust what the female was up to.

He sensed the change in air when the female shifted. With a howl, Chayton shoved the male off of him and spun, only he was too late. The female had snatched up one of the guns and pointed it at him.

A moving target was harder to hit. Fire lanced his gut as a blast rang out. She plugged two more into him. Chayton felt like his insides wanted to heave out of his mouth. He staggered midstep and dropped. His face hit the ground. With his last threads of energy, he turned to Kaitlyn.

She grunted and threw the male off of her. His limp form landed with a thud, the silver finally doing him in.

Kaitlyn...

Fuzziness bordered Chayton's vision. The last image he saw was Kaitlyn's body jerk one, two, three, four times. The rogue emptied the clip into his mate. She stumbled back. He feared she'd tumble over the edge, hoped she did to get away.

Chayton's mind swelled to bursting. He realized he was screaming her name.

A familiar howl sounded in the distance. Chayton fell quiet, like his body had, there was not enough blood left pumping through his veins. His lids drifted shut.

He sensed the rogues, but heard scuffling and a splash.

"Let her go," a gruff voice said. The remaining male must've shifted. "We'll take this one and make him pay. She'll come find us and we can finish her off."

Rough hands grabbed Chayton and hauled his body up. He didn't let blackness claim him until it registered that Kaitlyn had gotten away.

***

A warm nose nudged her chin.

Kaitlyn batted it away, mumbling something, but her words came out garbled. Had she been sucking on pennies? The copper taste overwhelmed everything.

A sound like gentle waves lapping on the shore surrounded her. Then a whine and more of that damn nose nudging her.

"What?" She groaned and tried roll over. Rocks dug into her side. Waves and rocks. Where was she?

The last moments before she blacked out hit her. Shot with her own weapon. Throwing her gear into the lake, but she'd fallen in after it.

What a fucking coward. Her intention had been to keep any more of her gear from being used against them, but she'd ended up abandoning Chayton to those heartless bastards.

Then who was nudging her?

She peeled her eyes open.

It was dark. She'd been out for hours.

I pulled you onto the shore.

The unfamiliar male's voice entered her thoughts. It wasn't unwelcome, just strange. Her gaze landed on him and widened. She choked back a startled yell. The white shifter she'd seen on the first day of this cursed mission towered over her. Bigger than any wolf she'd seen, with a hunched stance because he was more like a cross between a furred man and a wolf. Like a werewolf.

"You're the ancient? Cian?" Her voice came out hoarse.

He ducked his head. *I followed you from Valley Moon, but I was too late.*

She blinked. "Why?"

You have a vehicle. He sat down, but it didn't decrease his size any.

"No. Why did you follow me?"

This time he blinked and looked away. *You look like your mother.*

She sat up and immediately regretted it. Searing pain ping-ponged through her insides. How many times had she been shot?

Four. Not all of them and had gone straight through and she was left with the lead buried in her body. Irritating and painful, but something she could work around.

"Wait. You knew my mother?"

He didn't say anything and his expression remained placid.

"It doesn't matter right now. I have to get to Eagle. They have him, don't they?"

He inclined his head. She rolled to her hands and knees to stand. She needed food to replace all the blood she lost.

Eat.

A pile of fresh rabbit carcasses laid nearby. She'd been out long enough for Cian to hunt after he pulled her out of the water.

It was thoughtful. Her stomach rumbled. To help Chayton, she'd eat every one of these suckers raw.

Eat. And I'll explain.

Kaitlyn crawled to the heap of fur. She withdrew a blade from the damp holster secured around her thigh. She wondered if she could get her guns working. Had the water destroyed the silver-wash on the bullets?

Probably.

She sighed and skinned her first rabbit. Instead of rebelling, her mind rejoiced at the food supply. Shifters lived a long time, she couldn't avoid raw meat forever.

Wielding her knife, she carved off several pieces and popped them into her mouth. Cian watched. Funny how she felt comfortable around him. Her thoughts danced over what she'd do next. Recover her gear, follow the trail to Chayton, pray he was still alive.

They'll torture him first.

Her heart sank. Yeah, she'd guessed that if he wasn't dead, life wasn't pleasant.

You need reinforcements.

"I don't have time."

It's either reinforce or die once you find him.

"It'll take the Guardians at least a day to get here and that's after the hours it'll take me to get back to the colony."

The colony is full of fierce fighters. The rogues said they were using him to lure you to them.

She cut into her second rabbit, hunger driving her hard. Going to the colony was a smart option, but time wasn't on her side.

Raw meat wasn't as terrible as she assumed. Her human expectations had blocked a natural act.

"Why can't you help? They seem to be terrified of you."

He swung his shaggy head away. *I cannot.*

"Why?"

He turned with a warning stare. *I just can't.*

She was struck by his eyes. Such a clear green. So familiar.

"While I'm eating, tell me how you know my mother."

He grew introspective again and gazed across the waves reflecting pale moonlight. *I go into civilization sometimes when the urges get to be too much. It was a one-night stand.*

Kaitlyn paused, her knife hovered over the carcass. Her mom cheated on her dad with *Cian*?

The meat in her belly suddenly wasn't sitting so well. Her mom had cheated on her dad with Cian.

I had no idea it'd be anything more. I never saw her again. But your scent doesn't lie.

No.

I have a child who lives in Valley Moon. It's why I stay close. Your scent is very much like hers, and your mother's.

"Shifters aren't supposed to be able to reproduce outside of mating."

There are anomalies, and apparently, I am one. I have had at least two children a century that I know of. You and my other daughter are the only survivors.

Her meal churned in her belly. "Why do they all die?"

Did she have some weird genetic disease? Was that what was really behind her faulty shifting?

Various reasons. Mostly violence. And here you are, a Guardian. He gave a long blink. A child born for fighting.

His mournful words roused her defensive nature. "And that's a bad thing?"

In my life, yes. How's your mother?

Kaitlyn glared at him, unsure whether she should be angry at him for asking. "Dead."

His eyes closed. *I'm sorry.*

She knew she didn't have to tell him, but she needed an outlet for her sudden rage. "My dad killed her when I hit puberty and shifted and he realized she must've been unfaithful."

Cian's head dropped. *I'm sorry. It's why I remain alone. Those around me end up getting killed or die because of me.*

His mournful, heartfelt words hit home. Damn her soft heart. "Look, I know it wasn't your fault. You didn't pull the trigger." She forced herself to choose a third rabbit, the fuel necessary to help Chayton. "Why did Mom do it? Was she out looking for someone else?"

She wasn't. She was out for a hike and so damn beautiful, and sad. I felt a kinship with her, but I tried to stay away. I took my human form and went swimming. She found me and we started talking. He drifted off to stare into the distance, a trait that seemed too common for him. *I wanted more time with her, but she was determined to return to your father.*

"Yeah, that was her problem." Kaitlyn wondered how much heartache could've been saved if her mom had left her controlling dad. Would his jealous streak have pursued her only to hurt her?

She sliced off one more chunk. The fur pelts laying in a pile made her think of Chayton and how he would've saved them. She'd seen him giving his furs to a specialty shop in West Creek that processed them and made products to sell. *Waste no part of the animal*, he often said snidely. She'd always asked if he bedazzled his bathroom tile with fish scales.

She smiled sadly. His sneer had never hidden the smile in his eyes at her teasing. Why did he try to scare her off over and over?

She'd never know if she didn't go save his ass.

Chapter Eight

Pain radiating from all of his extremities lured Chayton back to consciousness. He wanted to dive back into the darkness to escape it, but his survival instinct prodded him to wake. This time he may be able to maintain alertness.

He didn't open his eyes, but used his other senses. He was still outdoors. Did his captors not have a survival pit they festered in? A cave?

"Open your eyes, Guardian," the female rogue sang in his ear. Her raspy voice was either natural or from howling or hollering. A female with multiple males descending into feralness probably spent a lot of time calling out in pain. He didn't pity her, doubted she was a victim. All her actions indicated a willing participant.

"If I open my eyes, would I have to look at your ugly muzzle?" His words were garbled but clear enough.

A fist smashed his nose. Warm blood oozed down his cheek. Amazing he had enough blood left to bleed. He added a throbbing face to the long list of poorly healing wounds covering his body. He tugged on each limb, but he was secured, his arms and legs spread out and anchored around a tree. Did they steal these supplies or did they have someone leaving them a pile of rope in the forest with their steaks? "Sorry, I didn't realize you were sensitive about your looks. Is that why you couldn't live in society anymore?"

Another fist clipped his chin this time. His teeth clattered, but at least he didn't bite his tongue.

One of the males chuckled. Chayton pried his lids open and found the three surviving rogues surrounding him. Sweet Mother, this was going to hurt.

The pale one spoke. "You embody the reason why we left our colony in the first place. Self-centered arrogance." He stalked closer and twisted Chayton's hair into his fist. "This symbolizes what a powerful warrior you are, no?"

Chayton glared at him. If they thought a haircut would make him cry, they had it wrong. His hair would grow back, these rogues' intelligence wouldn't.

The male leaned down and bared his fangs. "In fact, I think we should take all the parts of you that make you think you're a man and better than us. Do you think this hair and that floppy dick are what makes you fit to rule us?"

What? How did they know he was primed as the next leader of Spirit Moon after he mated with Tika? They were being supplied by Chayton's colony with more than physical gear. But why information?

The female stepped between his legs, brandishing a wicked blade. Chayton strained against his ropes, the blond shifter yanked his head tight. Getting each strand of hair pulled out one by one seemed like a vacation compared to what he guessed the female planned.

Castration.

Fuck, his balls would grow back, but how much would that hurt? Unless she cut them off. Shifters' healing capabilities stopped at regenerating body parts. That'd solve his problem with Tika. She'd gladly release him from his vow if he showed up missing pieces. He would chuckle at the irony if the thought of losing his manhood wasn't so traumatizing.

She grabbed his sac, her laughing eyes signaled the male at his head. Chayton dimly wondered what the third had planned for him when the blade struck.

Blinding agony hit him like lightning. Ropes cut into his wrists and ankles, he gritted his teeth so hard his fangs would've punctured his lower lip if his mouth wasn't drawn tight in a silent scream. And silent it was. Chayton wasn't gifting them by broadcasting any more pain than the stifling torment rolling off him in waves.

His head fell back against the ground. A hunk of ink-black hair hung from the male's hand. The knife between his legs stabbed him again. White-hot pain lanced his groin. Chayton would've thrown up if he'd had anything in his belly.

"Time for a close shave." The shifter's dark laugh was the last thing Chayton heard before he gladly let darkness sweep him back under.

***

"Des!" Kaitlyn sprinted to the cabin. She sensed his presence, so she kept yelling. "Des! I need a phone."

Des crashed through the patio door and as soon as he saw it was only her, screeched to a halt. "Where's Chay?"

"The rogues captured him. They're using him for bait. I need the colony's best fighters to follow me."

Des was turning to go, but he stopped and swiveled back. "I'll rally our warriors, but they won't follow you anywhere. You're not one of us."

Kaitlyn wiped sweat off her brow and stalked past Des into the house. "I don't give a fuck what they think." She found Chayton's spare items by the couch and dug out his phone. "And Des, I want warriors *you* trust. There's shifters in this colony helping the rogues."

Des bristled. "Why would they do that?"

"Exactly." She punched in the commander's number. It rang once before he answered. She filled him in; Des listened intently.

"Anyone there you can trust to have your back?" Commander Fitzsimmons asked.

~138~

She cocked an eyebrow at Des, who inclined his head. "Yes."

"Call after you get him." The commander cut the line.

Des's speculative gaze didn't stop her mechanical motions loading up on gear. She wasn't going to waste time changing clothes. She smelled like lake water and dried blood from digging out the two bullets lodged in her side. As she checked ammo and strapped on holsters, she sensed no movement from Des. Without Des, she'd have to approach the colony's leader. "I'm leaving to find Mato as soon as I'm locked and loaded. Are you coming with or are you another ancient who refuses to fight?"

His gaze sharpened. "Cian's out there?"

"Yep, and while I'm grateful he saved me or I'd be hanging with the bottom-feeders in a lake, his pacifism pisses me off."

"You don't want Cian in a fight with you."

First, Des was just standing there. Second, he insulted her dad. She cleared that thought from her head. Her dad was the guy who rocked her to sleep, taught her to ride a bike, and let her dance on his toes. He was also the guy who killed her mother.

Kaitlyn drew the short straw twice in the dad department.

"Well, he refuses to fight, so it doesn't matter."

Des took a step forward, his expression severe. "I'm serious, Kaitlyn. I barely trust myself to go with you, but Chay's been my link to sanity. Cian's been toeing the feral line for centuries."

Kaitlyn huffed out a breath and straightened. Guns and knives resting against her hips and thigh comforted her. It was her new normal. "I don't sense any crazy from him, other than being a hermit."

"Those of us who survived the extinction barely did so with our minds intact. We lost nearly everyone. Those who had no one to begin with, like Cian, fared even worse, if they were unlucky enough to survive."

She charged out the door without bothering to see if Des followed or not. When she reached the driver's door of the SUV, she jumped. Des waited patiently by the passenger door.

Once they were settled, Kaitlyn threw the gearshift in reverse and stomped on the gas. "Hasn't Cian ever had a mate?"

"Rumor has it he did, but she never bonded with him—refused to bind her soul with his. Ancients don't need the ceremony to connect their souls to their mates, not like modern shifters. It's even easier for us, but she refused regardless, or because of, perhaps."

Kaitlyn snorted, earning a sidelong glance from Des. Mates who didn't want to bond must be a family curse. "Then how's he not bat-shit if he's never mated?"

Des rested his head against the headrest. "Guilt holds the worst of us in stasis, neither succumbing to the feral call, nor moving beyond to a fulfilling life."

"What does Cian have to be guilty for?" Other than knocking up her mother, who'd been married at the time.

"Differentiating between friend or foe is impossible for him during a fight."

Nice. Another dad who goes berserk. Kaitlyn jerked the wheel for a sharp right. Des gripped the oh-shit handle but otherwise said nothing about her driving. She sensed his urgency to help Chayton matched her own, but he hid it slightly better.

She sped through town and screeched to a halt in front of the colonial home of Mato. Zitkana poked her head up from where she was cleaning out the flowerbeds to ready them for winter. Kaitlyn left the engine running when she hopped out and charged up the front walk.

"Where's Mato?"

Concern highlighted Zitkana's eyes as she took in Kaitlyn's urgency and Des's shadow behind her. "Des?"

Kaitlyn rolled her eyes. Nothing pissed her off like old-school shifters. Strapped down with weapons, holding the title of Guardian, and the female still looked to a rumpled ancient for answers. The older shifter's assessing gaze barely concealed how she'd deemed Kaitlyn unworthy to breathe Spirit Moon's air. She hoped Zitkana got fleas.

Kaitlyn charged into the house. She followed her senses of where Mato could be. If Chayton's life wasn't in danger, she'd be irritated with him for leaving her to ask Mato for help.

As she burst through the door, Mato was already rising. A gorgeous female with lustrous black hair and a sundress stood beside the desk. Kaitlyn guessed the female was close to the same age as her.

"Explain," Mato barked.

"I need you to gather three of your best warriors to go with me into the forest."

Mato straightened and crossed his arms. His brown eyes flashed. "Why?"

She grudgingly admitted that he had the right to know. "Chayton's been captured by the rogues. Three are still alive."

The girl gasped. Kaitlyn didn't spare her a glance.

A sneer twisted Mato's lips. "Where were you when he was taken?"

Kaitlyn plastered her hands on the desk and leaned forward. With males like Mato, there were only two approaches. Completely appealing to their sense of authority or proving her balls were as big as theirs.

"Not that I have to tell you, but I was shot and lying at the bottom of the lake." She cocked her head at him. "I've never had to hunt rogues before who were so well-equipped by the colony."

Mato's nostrils flared. If possible, he grew in height. "Don't make accusations you can't prove, little girl. *No one* from this colony would aid rogues."

"I'll make the accusation again, and this time I won't stutter. Shifters from your colony are supporting the rogues, who are using Chayton as bait. Now I'll say it slower this time. I need three of your most trusted warriors."

The female sidled next to Mato and laid her hand on his arm. "Daddy, my mate needs help."

Kaitlyn's brow furrowed. Didn't the girl just hear that there was a Guardian in danger? Couldn't begging her dad to help her mate wait until after Kaitlyn left?

The girl's luminous amber eyes beseeched Mato. "Chayton's made me wait this long to mate, I couldn't stand it if he was killed before we took our vows."

Kaitlyn blinked at the girl. Blinked again. Her mind locked the pieces into place until the puzzle they formed finally made sense. The girl and Chayton planned to mate?

"What?" Kaitlyn cursed herself. This should wait until her mission was over. But—Chayton and this girl?

Mato patted his daughter's hand in reassurance. "Tika and Chayton are slotted to mate this spring."

Des inched up behind Kaitlyn. He still hadn't said a word, and for that Kaitlyn was grateful. She felt support from him and she needed it.

"I thought…I thought…aren't mates destined?" Kaitlyn cursed the question as soon as she asked it.

Mato cut her a sharp glance. "It *was* meant to be. Our bloodlines should be merged." He rose to loom over Kaitlyn. "Fine, you need three warriors. You've got me. Des?"

Des inclined his head in confirmation. Mato barked for Zitkana.

His mate appeared within seconds. "Get me Trevon."

Zitkana disappeared. Kaitlyn hadn't quit gaping at the revelation. Without revealing that she was Chayton's mate, Kaitlyn wanted some goddamn answers.

"Why did Chayton get stationed with us if his," she involuntarily choked on the word, "*mate* lives here?"

Tika ran her hands down her impossibly shiny hair. "He insisted we wait until I was twenty-five. We settled on this spring, although being holed up with him for the winter sounded good to me."

Kaitlyn's jaw clenched. Tika's tone spoke of familiarity between the two.

The female came around the desk. "I know he can take torture, but they won't kill them, will they?"

"As soon as they see us, they will." Kaitlyn forced calm, even breaths. At least the shifters in the room—except for Des, who must suspect the relationship between her and his son—assumed her roiling emotions were from Chayton's capture.

They waited in tense silence for Trevon to arrive. Kaitlyn used the time to work through her feelings. Hunting rogues while battling jealous, shunned girlfriend emotions would only get her, and possibly others, killed. A tickle feathered the edge of her mind. She brushed it off. Her focus was pinpoint.

That bastard. He'd belittled her, been ashamed of her history, and he'd been promised to another this whole time.

Long inhale. Longer exhale. He was supposed to be her mate and he treated her like that? He couldn't have made the promise to Tika after he met Kaitlyn, but he certainly didn't put a stop to it. Because it circled back around to Kaitlyn's history. It wasn't one he could be proud of.

She wasn't proud of what her dad did to her mom. She wasn't proud of her birth father, who didn't stick around long enough to know she existed. But she was damn proud of everything she'd accomplished and especially where she was at now. If that was the only thing she had going for her, so be it.

Who needed a man, anyway?

Her heart said she needed Chayton, but she'd give herself time. It wasn't every day she got deeply hurt and insulted. But as far as she was concerned, she had a mission to save a fellow Guardian. Once those rogues' hearts ceased beating, she'd go back to West Creek and keep doing her job. It'd save her sanity like it had before.

A male approached. Kaitlyn spun and eyed him. Tall, with the typical features of the predominantly Native American community, his clean, guileless scent hinted at his honor and loyalty. Mato's choice was a good one. She was briefing him on the mission when the male she remembered as Thomas stormed in.

Thomas glared at Mato, his fists clenched. "What's going on in the colony, Mato?"

"None of your business." Mato ignored the male like he was no more important than a bug.

Thomas pointed to Kaitlyn. "Guardians show up with no announcement from you. Then I get word you're demanding one of my pack without consulting me?"

Mato's expression turned menacing. "*I* am leader. I don't need your permission."

Thomas's brown eyes flicked between Kaitlyn and the male he obviously reviled. "We deserve to know what's going on."

"When I decide you need to know, you'll know." Mato's arrogance overwhelmed Thomas's anger.

"You don't always make the best decisions for your people."

"But they're my people. Leave us."

Thomas's nostrils flared and his lips twitched like he wanted to bare his fangs.

"Thomas," Mato snapped. "Challenge me for once or get out. Otherwise, I'll rip your throat out."

With hate in his eyes, Thomas stalked out, his posture so rigid Kaitlyn suspected he was under Mato's influence.

No one said a word, but Kaitlyn was grateful it'd been a brief confrontation.

Good a time as any to make her announcement. "I'm staying in human form." The males started to argue, but she held up a hand to silence them. There was that pesky tickle again. Suspicion grew. Was Mato trying to interfere, or was it residual emotions from Thomas's outburst? "I'm in charge."

"Guardian," Mato's brows lowered to glare at Kaitlyn. "This is my colony."

He'd made that clear and she'd have to be clearer. Kaitlyn pounded the top of the desk. Tika jumped, much to Kaitlyn's satisfaction. "I am a Guardian. For this mission, I am in charge. One of those rogues is dead because of my shooting. I have silver-laced bullets that will take out a shifter faster than teeth or claws." She slapped the bowie knife strapped to her thigh. "This will behead a shifter faster than teeth or claws. Just make sure you don't slow me down."

She paused to glare at all of them one by one. One thing she'd learned in her few years as a Guardian was that colonies like this thought of fighting in terms of four legs and fangs.

When she got to Des, she saw the gleam of approval in his gaze.

Trevon glanced at Mato before nodding. Kaitlyn pushed past him to storm outside. "I'll drive us the edge of town, where you'll shift. And," she stopped and spun, "if any one of you runs off ahead of me, thinking to take over this yourself, I'll plug silver in your ass before you go a hundred yards. Understand?"

Mato's thunderous expression satisfied Kaitlyn on a deeply personal level, but not as much as the fear of Kaitlyn in Tika's eyes.

Chapter Nine

Someone was touching him and it wasn't Kaitlyn. He hated passing out and being at their mercy, but he dreamed of a redhead with emerald eyes.

Did she get out of the lake?

"We didn't find your partner's body," the female purred and stroked his brow. "We're patiently waiting. While you're here, why not enjoy your time."

Had he mumbled out loud? He gave her a sidelong glance. Was she coming on to him? Did she really think he could get it up after she'd castrated him three times already? His balls hadn't fully grown back and all Chayton felt from his nethers was fire and agony. It was a constant struggle not to dry heave.

She petted his bald head. Her hand bumped over scabs and slices, proof of his decreased regenerative ability. Neither of the male rogues would get hired on as a barber, not with Chayton's recommendation.

"I could get it up if I had a little water." He could barely get the words out. They not only starved him, but withheld all water. His vision was constantly fuzzy, his body never regaining adequate healing ability.

Her sinister laugh sank all of Chayton's hope to soften her. "I wasn't talking about that kind of fun. Although," she trailed her fingers over his mangled ball sac until he flinched and jerked against his binds, "I'm sure you'd be an admirable lover. Does that little Guardian know what this can do?"

He tried not to react, but his sluggish mental control wasn't enough to keep him from tensing.

The female chuckled. "Oh yes, she does." She sat back on her haunches. "Good. Then she'll come for you. Your death will send a message to the Guardians that we'll pick you all off one at a time."

"The colony will stop you."

Would she reveal anything? Would Chayton be alive to tell anyone?

Her guffaw bounced off the trees. "The colony is next. Mato rules with an iron fist. Or should I say an iron mind?" Her face twisted in a sneer. "That bastard controls everyone with a thought."

He frowned, which in his state meant his mouth only twitched. He knew Mato's ability was some sort of mental influence, but Chayton had underestimated it. Mato had never used it on him. Chayton had wanted him to when he was younger and testing out his abilities. A good thing he hadn't. Mato had known a young and brash Chayton would've turned it around on him to see how far he could take it. The fallout of doing that to a leader might've gotten his family kicked out, or worse.

Could Mato be that strong to alienate his own people? Rogues weren't known to be individuals one could reason with. As the madness set in, it amplified baser drives like entitlement, resentment, anger. It was hard to say if they became rogues because of Mato, or in spite of him.

"Why didn't you go to the Guardians?" The words almost stuck around his drying tongue and parched throat.

"Guardians? Why didn't we notify them?" she clarified. When he managed to nod his head, she rolled her eyes to the treetops. "Seriously? When everyone knew *you*, a Guardian, were influenced into mating his daughter?"

Influenced? Chayton groaned. Keeping his ability under wraps must have fooled everyone in thinking he was susceptible to Mato, too. It might still be useful if the rogues tried to use any of theirs on him. If they *had* any useful abilities. Chayton hadn't seen them display anything. Their main talent right now was insanity.

"I'm tired of talking." The female flipped up a blade and grinned wickedly.

Chayton sighed and ignored her. The pain would start soon enough. He gazed through the trees towering over him. A white speck drifted down to land on his cheek, followed by another.

Snow. An inhale told him nothing about the weather. His senses were shot until he could recover fully. More flakes dotted his face, his bare abdomen. He welcomed the cold until the blade cut a line of fire into his stomach.

***

Kaitlyn surged over a crest and leaped to tuck and roll down the countryside. Sweat dampened her shirt, but the early winter air cooled her off. The weather was as warm as it was going to get in late afternoon this time of year.

She batted snow out of her eyes. How much of the white stuff were they going to get? Like any shifter, she could sense major weather events, but her concentration wasn't on the atmosphere. Any more snow and the ground would get slippery for her, a factor she hadn't planned for. Grimly, she figured she could always shift if needed.

Cian trailed them. Would she ever tell anyone the ancient was her father? For fuck's sake, she even had a sister.

Kaitlyn's lungs burned as she ascended another steep incline. She'd made up her mind to look up her half-sister and hope she wasn't a bitch. On the hunt for rogues after learning she was officially dumped before she even formed a relationship with her mate had showed her what she was in for if she didn't use her support system. Turning out like the rogues she hunted, her mind descending into a feral state, was not an option. But she had her pack and that was it. It's not like she could approach her human aunt and uncle. But she had a shifter sibling and father. That meant she needed to allow Cian into her life and pray he didn't go crazy and kill her.

She reached the top. The shifters accompanying her spread out to each side and jumped. The ground was wet enough to kick her feet out from under her. She twisted and rolled with it, comfortable with her agility, grateful to save face in front of the males.

I smell him, Des announced. The ancient's senses were more acute than hers.

It started with a faint taint to the air. Chayton's blood and pain. Several more steps and she ran into a cloud of his torment.

No matter how he'd hurt her with his rejection, he didn't deserve that much torture. At least his death didn't linger in the air.

Fall back, she ordered.

The wolves stumbled to a stop. Mato, no surprise, had the hardest time listening to her.

The snow will help mask our scent. Kaitlyn tasted the air. *Mato and Des, circle to the right and keep low. We don't know if all three of them are in one spot. Trevon, you're with me.*

Kaitlyn trusted Des to keep Mato in line. The ancient deferred to Mato, but she suspected it was only because he didn't care otherwise. With Chayton in danger, Des would make sure Mato didn't fuck it up.

She glanced at Trevon. His tongue lolled out from the exertion, but he gave her a solemn nod. No wonder Mato trusted him. Kaitlyn barely knew him and she trusted him, too.

Move out. She trotted in the opposite direction of the other two. Chayton's scent grew stronger. Sounds of fornication filtered through the trees, the smell of sex filled the air. She drew in a sharp breath. No, nothing but blood from Chayton.

They're going to be distracted. She blew snowflakes off her face. It was coming down heavier now. Getting stranded in the forest would hinder them, but they'd have the advantage as shifters, as long as injuries were at a minimum.

Kaitlyn withdrew the gun at her hip. The heft felt weird, but it was Chayton's weapon. Using it felt intimate. A pang of regret hit her, but she pushed it out of her mind. If this mission went well, she'd have her whole long life to regret letting things go too far with Chayton.

We have eyes on them. Des sounded serious, but she could determine nothing else. *One male and the female are copulating against a tree in human form. I can't see Chayton yet.*

Hold your position until we find Chayton. Trevon and I will keep going.

We can take them out now, Mato growled.

And the third rogue can gut Chayton and carve out his heart, Kaitlyn retorted. *Hold your position.*

A fading rumble was the only acknowledgement she got from him.

Trevon looked back at her over his shoulder. She motioned for him to swing out further to widen their search.

It worked. Chayton's scent was stronger, but weaker at the same time. Kaitlyn hadn't experienced a dichotomy like that: his blood and pain surrounded her, but his naturally strong life force was draining from constant abuse.

I see him. Trevon stopped behind a tree trunk and crouched down. *He's been drawn and not quite quartered. A male stands over him, waiting.*

Weapons?

He's armed with blades and guns.

Kaitlyn swore to herself. They were probably hers from the lake, dammit. Cian hadn't dragged them in and she assumed she'd get back to recover them. She hoped they jammed.

Two more males and a female sit in a circle behind him, naked and ready to shift.

Shock choked her. *What?*

Mato and Des both cursed through their mental connection.

I thought you said there were only three, Mato accused.

And I told you that they were getting help from your colony. Fuck. Kaitlyn ran the odds. She and Trevon could take out the most immediate threat to Chayton. But fighting four more? Mato and Des would take care of their two rogues within minutes and race to help, but what damage would be done in between?

Guess she'd find out. *I'll take out the sentry over Chayton with a silver-laced bullet. Trevon, as soon as I shoot, you charge and I'll cover. When I pull the trigger, I'll signal you and Des. Incapacitate them and find us. We'll take care of the fallen after they're all subdued.*

She bent to loosen her boots, then unhooked her shirt. She had a feeling she'd end up getting furry before the night was over.

I think you should strip altogether.

She shot a sharp look at Trevon, but his tone was respectful, professional. *Loose clothing will only be a detriment.*

Shifters ran warmer, but undressing in the cold didn't promise a pleasant experience. With stealth, she undid all her weapons and gently placed them on the ground. Next, her clothes came off. She'd never undressed so quietly and that included the times when she was a teenager and snuck guys into her room.

Retrieving Chayton's gun that she'd loaded with the deadly bullets, she calmed her thoughts. Step-by-step, she moved soundlessly through the snow closer to Trevon. Cold snow covered her feet, but her stress-filled veins kept them from going numb.

Nothing's changed, he spoke to her mentally. *They're joking about what they've done to Chayton and taking bets on who can cut his heart out.*

Kaitlyn shivered. She'd sever their arms before they got close to his heart. As she crept closer, the scene came into view.

She swallowed the growing lump in her throat. There wasn't a section of skin on Chayton not covered in blood. Including his bare scalp. So, they had sought to humiliate him, too. A great majority of the blood centered on his genitals.

Rowdy laughter drew her attention to the nude group behind the prisoner.

"I say we castrate him for real," one male called.

The rogue standing over Chayton shook his head. "We want his balls to grow back so we can keep slicing them open. We filleted his junk twice now."

The female spit. "I say cut his lips off. I'd love to never see that arrogant smirk again."

"Nah," the male replied, "we'll save the lip job for Mato."

They were distracted. She raised her weapon and put the male with the knife in her sights. Slow breath in. Snowflakes landed on her nose; she blinked them off her lashes, ignored the chill in the air and on her feet. Slow exhale. Pause at end of breath, add pressure to the trigger.

She released the mental command. *Go*.

The gun fired.

Right between the eyes. The rogue dropped.

The other three jumped up, but Kaitlyn had already sighted on one of the males. Before he shifted, she felled him, too.

Trevon charged the remaining two. Echoing snarls met his. The two other shifters ignored Chayton, which worked in Kaitlyn's favor.

She took aim, but Trevon had moved into the line of fire. Shit. The gun hit the ground, Kaitlyn flowed into her wolf, embraced the kick of heat it gave her, and took off.

Trevon engaged the female. The male was in a midair leap onto Trevon's back when Kaitlyn hit him from the side. They both thudded to the ground and skidded on the snow-touched surface. She couldn't spare a glance at Trevon, but the female was yelping and he was growling. A good sign that his jaws were engaged.

Kaitlyn rolled and sprang to all fours, but the male beat her. He lunged and clamped his jaws around her neck. She snarled at the stabbing fire of his fangs and shook her head, spinning to throw him off balance. It wasn't her quick reflexes that made him lose his footing but the slick ground.

Kaitlyn tumbled with the male, but twisted the other direction. He disengaged, but a hunk of her flesh went with him. She let out a yelp. Her blood joined the cloud of copper in the air. She whirled on the male. He was almost back to standing. She attacked, but slid on the pool of blood gathering under her.

The male bared his fangs as if laughing at her. She snapped out a paw and gouged his side. Instead of jerking back, he leaned into her hit. Her claws dug deeper, but he got closer. If he was going to play that game, she would, too. Flinging out another paw, she slammed her claws into his hide and tugged him close. He couldn't fight the Velcro effect of her grip. Her hind feet sliced into his belly. He howled and buckled over. She pulled him close, avoided his snapping jaws, and closed her jaw around his neck.

Warm blood seeped around his fur into her mouth. She rabbit-kicked him again with her hind legs while sawing her jaw back and forth for the greatest damage possible. They pushed and skidded over the ground. Her back rammed against a tree trunk; she used it for leverage. The male couldn't quit slipping, his movements growing weaker.

Kaitlyn! I can't move.

What?

Trevon didn't reply. Her neck throbbed. She resisted closing her eyes against the pain. She had to finish him to get to Trevon. The male thrashed, but his power drained quickly. Kaitlyn's mouth filled with blood, but not enough to drain his energy. The damage to his gut must be the reason.

"Stop," a female's voice commanded.

Kaitlyn tried to whip her head toward the sound, but her teeth were locked into the male. A brief touch against her mind, so similar to what she'd felt earlier, but it was gone. She pried her mouth off the male and kicked his limp body away. She flipped to face the female who stood above her in human form.

The other shifter drew her lips back. "I said *stop*."

There was the sensation in her head again. No time to think. Kaitlyn jumped up. Shock registered on the female's face before Kaitlyn tackled her. In her human form, the rogue shifter couldn't compete with Kaitlyn's ability.

Her jaw was tired, but she targeted the vulnerable neck again, an even better target on a human.

The female screamed. She tried to push Kaitlyn away, but wasn't strong enough to stop her momentum. Kaitlyn didn't have to clamp on. She took a mighty bite and the female toppled with a gurgle.

Kaitlyn crouched and shuffled back, her flanks heaving. The female was done for, the male twitched to the side. They both deserved a silver bullet, but Kaitlyn didn't dare transition and leave herself vulnerable. Too many shifters counted on her.

She trotted over to Trevon's prone form, each step ricocheting through the wound in her neck. When she reached him, she thoroughly sniffed him, but detected no scent of death. From his position at the base of a tree, his distress over not being able to move was from a broken back before he'd been knocked unconscious.

The two males she'd shot were both dead. Head shots with silver, speedy and efficient. With a fortifying breath, she padded to Chayton. A layer of snow covered his body, giving his injuries the illusion of being less severe than they were. Shifters lived long and died hard, but constant, severe trauma where the body couldn't keep regenerating often resulted in death. Or so Kaitlyn had been told. She'd never witnessed it before and didn't want today to be the first time.

His chest barely rose with each breath. Old blood spotted the ground around him, some in large pools, and some splattered on the trees. He needed fuel, but could he heal enough to ingest it?

He will make it. Des appeared in the trees. His hulking, brown man-wolf streaked in blood, the thing of nightmares. The only difference from her dad was the color. Ancients looked terrifying, and perhaps during their time, they were. Now Des and Cian reminded her of the old black belts who used to come into the various dojos she'd worked in. They still had the skills, but had accepted that they would never be the fighters they used to be.

Those other two are dead? she asked.

I ripped their hearts out myself.

Perhaps Des hadn't lost as much ability as Kaitlyn had assumed.

The gun to take care of the two shifters Trevon and I fought is laying by my things. Kaitlyn inclined her head toward the pile of gear hidden a couple hundred yards away.

Des considered her before he nodded. As he strode to retrieve the gun, he flowed to two legs. She turned her attention back to Chayton. Prowling up and down each side of his body, she determined the severity of his lingering injuries.

Still so strong, so proud. A jab of loss hit when she got to his head. His glorious hair had provided an intimate curtain when they were together. Logically, she knew it was only hair and it'd grow back. Only a silver blade would poison the hair follicles, but still, it'd take years to get that long again.

She'd like to be around to see it.

Mato ran to Chayton. *We can feed him as we carry him back. We'll take him to my place, where Tika can care for him.*

The female's name was a cold splash of reality.

We'll get him back for her. She was grateful for mental speak to keep her from gagging.

She spun away to check on Trevon, who was groaning. He flipped to his feet and scanned their surroundings.

The fight's over? You got her?

Des was coming back carrying all of her gear in one hand and the gun in the other. Kaitlyn wanted to see how he used it. Trevon seemed to want the time to gather his wits.

Des shot one bullet into each rogue. He lifted the gun to inspect it closer. *This is handy. Much easier.* He slipped it into her pack and lifted a questioning brow at her.

I can travel quicker in this form.

As always, Des seemed to sense more to her, like maybe he suspected her human upbringing caused certain deficiencies. Maybe, unlike his son, he didn't care and accepted her anyway.

Why couldn't *he* have been her father?

With the thought came a hint of Cian in the air. She squinted through the trees. The flash of white was difficult to distinguish in the falling snow, but her dad was out there.

She'd grudgingly accept his limitations, too. He didn't want to jump into the fight and rip out his own daughter's heart by accident. With her history, she'd respect that.

I will transport my son. Des shouldered her gear. Trevon transitioned to human to sever the bonds around Chayton's limbs.

He was so limp when Des lifted him across his shoulders. Kaitlyn firmly ordered herself to stay in place. She did her job as a Guardian. The rogues were dead, Chayton should recover, and Mato could deal with any lingering traitors in the colony.

We need to move to get back in time. She raised her head to sniff the wind. Travel when night was falling was far from ideal, but it was better than getting snowed out in the mountains. *The snow will slow us down, but we can be back to the colony by daybreak.*

Mato's mental snort raised her hackles. *If we're lucky.*

She bit her tongue, reminded herself that he'd helped her on the mission, and took off into the night. Her dad paralleled her. The others, so used to his random presence, didn't question it.

Chapter Ten

Chayton didn't want to open his eyes. Just breathing was agony. Pain lanced his lungs and each muscle protested at having to move as much as a centimeter.

A lush body pressed against him. Oh, yes. He could go for some of that. Flashes of red hair and creamy skin eased the pain.

He frowned. His genitals were unresponsive. Understandable after what they'd been through.

Wait.

He wasn't strapped down in the forest anymore. He inhaled, registering the familiar smells around him. He'd been to this place before, but he couldn't recall it immediately.

The female whose nude body curled into his trailed her fingers over his chest.

"Chay, are you finally awake?"

Oh, *shit*. He was at Tika's place. He'd only been there once, last year when he wanted to see how compatible they'd be. At the time, he'd thought they had a lot of potential.

He kept moving his lips around until it was possible to form words. "Kaitlyn?"

Tika lifted her head off his shoulder. "Your partner went home. I assured her I'd take good care of my future mate." She landed tiny kisses on his chest.

Chayton squeezed his lids tighter. He still hadn't opened his eyes, and now he wished he'd go back under to delay having to face the mess he'd gotten himself into.

"Was she—" he swallowed. When he'd last seen her, she'd been plugged with four rounds. "She was well?"

Tika propped herself up on an elbow. He finally opened his eyes. Hers widened in delight and she brushed her fingers over his cheek. "She was fine. After you were taken, she came and got Des and my dad. I guess she was injured in the rescue, but she was healed before they returned." Laughter burst from her, bouncing the bed. He winced at the sudden movement. "I guess she passed out when they got you back to the village and she had to shift back. Trevon had to carry her to Des's place."

A surge of propriety beat back his physical torment. Another agile, single male had his hands on his mate. Chayton should've been the one to be there to pick her up. Instead, she'd had to drag herself out of the lake and save his ass—then leave him.

Could he blame her? And it ended with her weakness displayed in front of Mato. Something about that male knowing her shifting disability made Chayton uneasy.

"Anyway…" She danced her fingers over his abdomen and down his hipbone. He flinched and she withdrew her hand. "You're snowed in and officially on vacation."

His eyes flew wide as he realized what she'd said. He surged up to a sitting position. Agony speared him and he didn't care. Dizziness spun the room, but his gaze anchored on Tika. "What do you mean?"

Her brow furrowed. "They barely made it back with you in the snow. It was noon the day after they left before they reached the colony. I guess once she came to, she packed everything and dropped your stuff over when she checked on you." Tika lifted her chin to point out his satchel and tactical gear. "Said she was going back to Valley Moon before snow accumulation blocked her in. She'll have an easier time getting back to West Creek from there. Their roads are cleared much earlier than ours."

Because Mato didn't think the colony needed access to civilization to survive; they owned one snowplow.

Tika reached for something on the nightstand. She handed the mug to him. "Drink."

He accepted the mug, his arm as weak as a newborn. It shook as he drained the salty broth, but he didn't know if it was from his injuries or his agitation.

Even if Kaitlyn didn't know he was her mate, she had to have experienced the strong drive of the mating call. He sure as hell had. What they'd done together, she had to feel like he'd slapped her in the face, repeatedly.

Sweet Mother, he'd fucked up. He'd fucked up twenty-five years ago when he caved under Mato and Zitkana's pressure and he'd nailed his coffin lid over the last week.

He'd need to be full strength to face reality. Sinking back down with a sigh and a moan, he closed his eyes. "Thanks," he mumbled before he drifted off.

***

Kaitlyn tapped her fingers against her other hand waiting for the door to open. She'd found the address Cian gave her easily enough. The tiny clapboard house sat on a postage stamp-sized lot on a long street with other similar houses, much like the neighborhood in Freemont she'd grown up in. Nervous energy had coursed through her body from the drive to Valley Moon. Snow had fallen steadily since Chayton's rescue. But she was determined to get away from his colony and the clingy Tika while she still could. The risk of driving through the winter storm was worth it. Drifts across the highway had created a few white-knuckled moments when she plowed over them and the SUV almost got hung up.

The door opened to a young woman, slightly younger than Kaitlyn, with pale blonde hair chopped off at the chin. Her green eyes flashed with curiosity as she studied Kaitlyn's appearance. Her name, Tawny, was a perfect fit.

The female's nostrils flared, studying Kaitlyn's scent. She spoke with no hostility, but no welcome. "Can I help you, Guardian?"

God, yes. Leaving Chayton shredded her. She wished she had a mirror to see if her eyes were still bloodshot from crying after making the mistake of turning on the radio to classic country. "Actually, I wanted to talk. May I come in?"

The female's eyelids fluttered in question, but she opened the door wider for Kaitlyn to step in. Several scents assaulted Kaitlyn. One was a scent so much like her own Kaitlyn almost didn't notice it. Another she almost missed it because this girl, her sister, had a characteristic scent, one Kaitlyn knew well.

Like a coward, Kaitlyn jumped on that topic first. "Why aren't you a Guardian?"

A guarded look shaded Tawny's expression. "My father requested I find a less violent path in life."

"You're not Cian."

"How did you—are you here to recruit me?" The spike of hostility in her sister's tone scared Kaitlyn that she'd get kicked out.

Kaitlyn sighed and stomped snow off her boots in case she was invited to stay. "No, I came because Cian is my father, too."

Tawny looked like Kaitlyn had felt when Cian told her.

Kaitlyn hooked her thumbs in her waistband and let it all spill out. "I don't have any family left and my mate chose another, so I'm kind of in a shitty spot right now."

Sympathy filled her sister's expression. Kaitlyn hadn't told half of her pathetic story, but Tawny sensed the anguish.

"And you're snowed in here needing a friend?"

Kaitlyn nodded and blinked back tears. What she wouldn't give to bawl on her bestie Cassie's shoulder and have a good sparring session with Jace, who'd add a word or two of wisdom, even offer to hunt down Chayton. "Once I found out about you, I planned to find you anyway."

Tawny opened the door to let Kaitlyn inside with a small smile. "We're kind of an oddity, huh?"

Kaitlyn hastily wiped her eyes. "Has it been bad for you?"

Tawny barked a laugh. "Sweet Mother, I'm miserable. My mom's a drunk because my dad won't mate her, and my dad wasn't here to raise me, yet I let him run my life." Her eyes widened and she put her fingers to her mouth. "I can't believe I said that."

Kaitlyn chuckled, relieved. "Have I got a story for you."

Chapter Eleven

Chayton prowled his father's home. After three days, he'd healed enough to escape to his dad's place. Hell with the weather, he couldn't lay in Tika's bed any more.

"Son, I didn't rebuild this house so you could wear a hole in the floor." Des sipped coffee at the tiny kitchen table and read a book.

"Doesn't Mato have the plow out?" Chayton slammed his own mug down for coffee. It cracked and he growled and tossed it. "It's been a week."

"What are you going to do when you get back?"

Good question. He needed to get out of city limits first. Rolling his shoulders, trying to loosen knots, he finally asked *Ahte* his burning question. "Why didn't you say anything all those years ago when Mato hounded me about Tika? Did you think it was a good idea?"

Des set his cup down. "Right after your mom told me what was going on with Mato and Zitkana hounding you, the fire claimed her." Lines creased his eyes, lending to his constant aura of sadness. For once, his father looked old. "Once she was gone, it was all I could do to remain on this earth for you."

"Why did you?"

"It wasn't easy. I wanted to find a deep hole and wither away. Even start my own fire. But once I discovered you swore yourself to Tika, I couldn't go." He grimaced and rubbed his chest. "I had this sense that it wasn't a good idea, that you'd need my help."

Chayton stabbed his boot into the floor. "Kaitlyn's my mate."

"I sensed as much. Mato won't let you go free."

Mato? Tika wouldn't let him go. Chayton scrubbed his face. Once he'd regained enough vitality to get out of bed, he dressed and grabbed his pack. Tika tried to seduce him back between the covers, but he used the excuse that he needed to talk to his dad and call his commander. In the days since he'd fully recovered, his mating bond screamed that he go after Kaitlyn.

He still had to call Commander Fitzsimmons. Kaitlyn likely already had, but he needed to touch base. Find out if he was welcome back to the pack.

"You've been with Tika already?" There was no censure in his dad's tone.

Chayton nodded.

"She didn't mark you. As tenacious as she seems, I would've thought she'd mark you. But it's not like she's been patiently waiting."

"What do you mean?"

"She fulfills her needs often." When Chayton shot him a sharp look, Des lifted a shoulder. "It's a small town. Sometimes my only amusement is gossip, though I do pay more attention to Mato and his family. They are affecting your life, and that concerns me."

Great. A year of abstinence for an unfaithful mate. To think he'd tried so hard to stay away from Kaitlyn, might have missed those stolen moments with her.

Chayton strode to the sliding door. The sun was high, its strong rays rapidly melting snow. "I made a blood vow with Zitkana. You really think they'll release me?"

"Mato's been a strong leader, but his age is catching up to him. He and Zitkana finally had a kid make it to adulthood, I don't blame him for trying to secure a future for her." Des shook his head. "I think you were targeted for your parentage, your Guardian connections, and, more importantly, because no one could undermine your authority. Not with your gift."

Chayton crossed his arms and watched water drip off the gutters. "So I can turn any shifter's ability around on them. What would I do with that?"

"Retain power, for Tika. She must have an ability, but I suspect that like her, it's not that strong."

He frowned. "If she can't retain authority when Mato dies or steps down, then she doesn't deserve the position."

"Says someone who's not a father."

"Mato's afraid Tika will inherit the position and get killed when she's challenged?"

"Targeting his children while he's alive hasn't proven fortuitous. There are enough shifters who back Mato. I think that's why no one's challenged him."

Chayton clenched his jaw. "Biding their time, weakening the colony."

He'd worried Kaitlyn's perceived weakness would be used against her, but it was Tika who was vulnerable. Other than her beauty and charm, there wasn't much to her.

"Exactly."

"Dammit, *Ahte*, quit reading my thoughts."

"Quit projecting them." Des stood and walked around the table. "I couldn't read Kaitlyn's."

Chayton let the information sink in. "Resistance to other's abilities is a unique gift. I assumed she hadn't come into them or possessed none."

"I've met one other who can do the same thing. Cian."

Chayton scoffed. What were the odds? "No."

"Yes, I believe so. He has another daughter in Valley Moon."

Kaitlyn's birth father could be an ancient. Chayton dropped his head as the irony smacked his ego. No braid hung down his back and his scalp felt like an air conditioner blew across it constantly. Most of the time he didn't notice he was a *natasla*, baldhead, because his thoughts were wrapped around a redhead.

He'd been such an ass. Not only did she have the bloodline of an ancient, but she'd saved his mangled hide, defunct shifting and everything.

"I fucked up so bad."

"We all do at some point." Des said, his tone sympathetic. He rose and walked out the door, barefoot, onto the damp deck.

Chayton followed. "I cursed having her as my destined mate."

"That was your mother's thinking. Proud to the bone of her heritage, and mine." He chuckled softly. "If I succumbed to that line of thinking, I would've turned feral long ago. I slept my way through every ancient female I could find. No mate. Decades passed and my envy grew of those who found their mates among humans. Once your mother crossed my path, I didn't care if she had the bloodline of a gnat, I wanted my mate."

"Thanks for making me feel like shit, *Ahte*."

Des clapped a hand on his shoulder. "You'll pass your Sioux blood down to your young no matter what. I'm more worried all your *ina's* native knowledge will be lost."

"Never." A lump formed in Chayton's throat. "She taught me everything and I remember it all."

"Good. Good. Perhaps, your mate will enjoy learning."

Would Kaitlyn allow him to teach her his traditions? Tika probably knew them all, but she held no appeal for Chayton.

**

"You sure you want to tackle the roads?" Tawny peered outside between the blinds. "The sun's been out enough to melt the roads, but it's still cold enough to turn it into a sheet of ice."

"I'll drive slow." Kaitlyn finished brushing her hair. Choosing a French braid, she started weaving the plait into her long hair. It was second nature after having worn it secured back nearly every day. She contemplated cutting it, and just like that, a scarred and bald shifter came to mind.

Tawny glanced over her shoulder. "You're thinking about him again."

"I didn't mean to."

Being stranded with Tawny had been just the vacation Kaitlyn had needed. A sister. Kaitlyn and her best friend, Cassie, had bonded like sisters when she was fostered by Kaitlyn's aunt and uncle. Kaitlyn hadn't dared hope the same would happen with Tawny.

Turned out the girl was just as desperate for someone who understood what it was like to be the progeny of Cian. Tawny had the gift of knowing who her father was her whole life, but it wasn't roses and lollipops.

"I can't believe he hasn't even called you." Her sister left the window to drape herself on the seat next to Kaitlyn.

"It's better that he hasn't." Hadn't even *tried.* No text, nothing. Argh. She should hate him, not fall into mournful longing whenever he crossed her mind.

"Sucks, though." Tawny tucked a short lock behind her ear. "Why don't you hack your hair off? It has to be a pain to braid every day."

"Short hair can get in my eyes, and if I trim it, part of it escapes when I tie it back."

"What if a bad guy grabs it?"

Kaitlyn smirked and her sister looked away. Tawny could ignore being destined to be a Guardian, but she couldn't escape her fighting instincts. Maybe she'd come around.

"I can tuck the tail back up and secure it if I'm worried, otherwise I'll just hack it off."

"Midfight?"

Kaitlyn snatched a knife from her ankle holster. Tawny's eyes widened as she tried to follow the sudden movement to where the blade rested next to Kaitlyn's partial braid. It wasn't shock that filled her gaze, but pure interest.

She'd come around. Kaitlyn knew the drive to protect and defend with no outlet. It's not a craving that would be satisfied until she was strapped with deadly metal ready to kick down the door of an abusive shifter.

"You can come with me back to the lodge, check the place out." Kaitlyn finished her hair and tied it off. "Cian doesn't control you, and now he knows about me, so maybe he'll feel differently anyway."

Tawny's expression waffled between running to her room and packing or planting her butt firmly on the chair. Kaitlyn rooted for having company for the treacherous drive home, and to have her sister enter training.

Resignation won. Kaitlyn silently cursed.

"There's still my mom to think about." A muscle twitched in Tawny's jaw as she glared at the door. "She won't give up on Cian when he's given up on her. It kills her every time he lures a female out to spend time with him."

Ugh. Was that Kaitlyn's future—living in the forest and luring sex partners out?

"I'd better go." She stood and grabbed her pack.

Tawny rose to embrace her.

Kaitlyn clutched her sister. She needed the life raft. "Thank you so much." Hell, tears burned to escape.

Tawny sniffled. "Thank you for finding me. Keep in touch."

"You're welcome to visit any time." *Please*.

"We could meet in Freemont, have a girl's weekend. Bring this Cassie you told me about, who kept you out of trouble."

Kaitlyn snorted. "She didn't keep me out of it, she kept me from getting caught." With a grin, she broke away. Outside, she stepped gingerly over the ice to the SUV.

Time to go back to normal life.

Chapter Twelve

She should've stayed in Valley Moon. Lord, the roads were as slick as a hockey rink. Creeping along the highway at twenty-five miles per hour meant she'd reach Freemont in an hour. Darkness approached and fluffy snowflakes hit the windshield with increasing frequency. Snow on top of ice in the dark while in the middle of the country, not a good combination.

Kaitlyn's alarm flared each time she thought the back wheels hinted at a fishtail. She hadn't thrown it in four-wheel drive yet. *Four-wheel slide*, her dad had always said.

What would Cian say? Four feet are better than wheels?

Crappy driving conditions meant Kaitlyn had a lot of time to ponder the new people in her life, and the person who'd left her.

Before she had left Spirit Moon, she'd checked on him. It was disconcerting to see his scars in such contrast to the gray pallor of his skin. Tika talked incessantly about how well she cared for Chayton, and Kaitlyn had left mid-sentence.

She flipped the wipers on and eased up on the gas pedal. Any slower and she might as well walk.

A brief sensation of weightlessness, then the vehicle drifted into the other lane. Kaitlyn let off the gas completely and turned the wheel in the direction she wanted to go. She hit a patch of dry pavement and jerked back into her lane, only to slide on another icy section. She couldn't correct in time and the SUV skidded into the ditch. Punching the gas and hitting the four-wheel drive button, she tried to plow out of the deep snow. Progress slowed until the wheels spun.

Motherfucker!

Kaitlyn slapped the wheel, but had to back off before she ripped it out. She threw the gearshift in reverse and slowly pressed the gas. The vehicle jerked, followed by the sound of wheels spinning. Put the gearshift in drive. Wheels spun. Reverse. No luck. Drive. Nothing.

She sighed. At least she'd get a workout shoveling.

Climbing out, she sunk into knee-deep snow. She tromped around to the back and lifted the hatch. The shovel lay on top as if it had known she'd need it.

Before she began, she called the commander and explained her situation. "So, I'm gonna be late."

"Get yourself out, get to town, and get a room. The snow won't quit until morning. Our roads are plugged and there's no rush for you to get back."

"Got it, sir."

At least two hours of hard shoveling had passed when her phone chimed. A surge of hope went through her that it might be Chayton. What would she say? Act neutral, pissed, or cool?

She wiped off her sweaty brow and pulled out her phone. Waylon?

"Hey, Guardian." His rough voice was a welcome balm to her ragged ego. "Whatcha doing tonight?"

She rested an arm on the shovel and held the phone to her ear with the other hand. Her shirt had been more than enough to keep the chill away while shoveling, but with fresh snow falling on her and her sweat evaporating, the cold was nipping at her exposed skin.

"I'm digging myself out of a ditch."

He chuckled. "Sounds like a killer of a night. Need me to help you warm up when you're done?"

A booty call. She kicked at the tire she'd been unburying. "I need a place to stay tonight that's not a dive." *If I can make it to town and not camp out here.* "Where do you think I should go, the Freemont Inn?"

His voice dropped low. "I think you should cross the river and stay with me."

She didn't reply, but thought hard about her answer. Would she turn Waylon away forever and explain why, or would she move on with her life like Chayton was going to do with Tika?

"I need a roof over my head tonight, nothing else. It's been a shitty couple of weeks."

"Come on over, Kaitlyn." Waylon's tone turned serious instead of flirty. "Save your money and come hang out. I've got leftover Chinese."

Laughter bubbled up. She'd never been to his place. They'd always met at Pale Moonlight to meet their needs, but he was an incorrigible bachelor who worked all the time. When he wasn't working, he trolled the clubs for willing bodies. She doubted he had time to cook a meal or decorate his pad.

Money wasn't an issue, but her inner rebel encouraged her. "Text me your address and I'll roll in as soon as I can roll out of the snowbank."

She disconnected and put her phone away. Why did she feel guilty? She needed a place to stay and she didn't plan on getting any action. Waylon was a friend first, bed buddy second. She was taking a friend up on an offer. Why'd it feel so wrong?

***

More snow. Any wind and it'd turn into an *iwoblu*.

Chayton spun away from the window. His *ahte* was out running and Chayton should've gone with him. Staying behind was supposed to be for thinking about what he was going to say to Tika. Everything sounded lame and he was more worried about Mato. Would he blow? Now that Tika was an adult, would he not care? Would Mato kick Des out of the colony, along with him?

Would they release him from the bond in the first place?

He eyed the phone he held. Kaitlyn's number was punched in; he just needed to hit send.

He tapped the green button and ignored the somersault in his gut.

She answered with a wary, "Hello."

"You okay?"

Her sigh of resignation cleaved through him. "Yeah, I am."

"Are you still in Valley Moon?"

"No, I left yesterday and made it to West Creek. I'll try to make it to the lodge today, but I think the snow will clog the route for at least another day. I don't feel like digging myself out again."

"Again. You went off the road?"

Before she could answer a male voice cut through the line. "Kaitlyn, want to grab some lunch before you head out?"

Chayton's fist's clenched. His phone gave under his grip. It'd crumple if he didn't ease up. "Who. *The fuck*. Is that?"

"I stayed at a friend's house last night."

His head threatened to explode. "Waylon." His voice bounced off the kitchen walls.

"Yes, but we didn't—" She made a disgusted sound. "You know what, it's none of your damn business. You chose Tika for your mate instead of me."

When her words registered, he stilled with shock. "You knew that we were supposed to be mates?"

"Of course. I'm a *shifter*. Regardless of what you think of me, I function like one."

"And you didn't say anything?" He shouldn't feel a sense of betrayal, but that didn't stop it.

"You made it obvious you didn't want me by the way you treated me." Her voice rose louder with each sentence. "You could've cut the bullshit, showed me some respect, and told me why. Instead you used it as an excuse to demean me. I wasn't good enough for you."

He opened his mouth to defend his actions, but she was absolutely right. The fact should've made him apologetic, but his mating instinct overrode good sense. "Did you fuck him?"

"Oh my god, Chayton. It's none of your business. When I left Spirit Moon, you were in Tika's bed, so *fuck off*."

She disconnected.

She was with a male. And she'd spent the night with him.

He slammed his phone down, otherwise he'd whip it at the wall. He flung his head back and he roared. Rage echoed off the walls.

When he was done, he was still alone, and still sworn to Tika. *Eya!* Kaitlyn could move on, so could he.

Chapter Thirteen

Tika opened the door with a surprised smile. "Hey, Chay. I didn't know you were coming to town."

She blinked at his glare. Chayton dragged in a breath to soften his gaze. He'd made himself wait a full twenty-four hours to approach Tika. Acting rash in the face of extreme emotion hadn't benefitted him in the past. "I thought we could talk."

"About?" She stepped aside to let him in.

"Us." Closing the door behind him, he considered his words. "What are you going to do if you meet your mate after we've bonded?"

"It seems really unlikely I'll meet him when I don't leave the village." She ran a hand through her long hair, a frown on her face, her eyes pensive.

She wasn't confident about committing to the eternity of a bond.

"Why haven't you told your parents you don't want to bond with me?" Was there a way out of this?

"I do want to be with you." She fiddled with the ends of her hair. "But maybe we don't have to bond fully. Like when I meet my mate, we can go our separate ways."

"Are you kidding?"

She rested her fists on her hips. "You swore yourself to me. I'm the only surviving child of this colony's leader."

"And?"

He was rewarded with a *duh* look.

"And you have the honor of protecting me so I can assume the leadership position."

Physically recoiling, he shook his head. "A leader shouldn't have to be *protected*. She should be able to handle herself in a fight."

She kicked her chin up. "I can."

He didn't know how to reply without bringing her to a fight involving Kaitlyn. Or hell, any other female that belonged to the West Creek Guardian pack. But he didn't have to reply.

Glass shattered as a body rolled through the picture window. Tika screamed and thrust her hands up. The fall of glass slowed. The shifter who surged through the window halted midroll. So, Tika *did* have a power, and thankfully, it was useless on Chayton. He charged the male just as her ability wore off.

He tackled the male shifter. A knife aimed for his gut. Chayton wrenched his arm to the side and cracked it against the couch. Bone crunched and the male yelped.

Chayton sensed another intruder. He strained to look over his shoulder for Tika. Two more males were charging her. She stood frozen with fear.

"Tika," Chayton roared. "*Move*."

A fist slammed into his jaw. He flew back. The male he'd been fighting jumped on him, pinning him down. One of the other attackers dove in to help.

"Help, Chayton!"

Chayton gritted his teeth as he fended off fists and knees. Silver glinted. Chayton let go of one attacker and yanked the wrist holding the knife down and to the side. Bone yielded as it snapped. He released and jammed his elbow into another male's nose. They must've thought that because they had him on the ground, they had the advantage.

A blow nailed him in the gut, forcing the air from his lungs. Chayton jerked his knees up and used one leg to wrap around a male neck. The shifter fought and beat at Chayton's legs. Chayton squeezed harder. He slapped away a lamp swinging toward him. Tika screamed. He smelled her blood in the air.

Enough playing around. He twisted his whole body, releasing the shifter only to stomp him in the face. Both he and the other male dove for one of the knives laying on the floor. Chayton beat him to it and rammed it to the hilt in the male's chest. Bonus. He hit the heart and the male dropped. He drew his gun and shot the first male in the head.

Spinning around, he found the third male was gone. Tika lay on the floor gripping her side. Blood seeped through her fingers. A gray pallor tinted her skin; she gasped for breath. Her mouth was moving, but he couldn't hear. Sinking to his knees, he focused on her mouth.

"S-s-silver."

Sweet mother. Ripping open the pouch on his belt, he snagged his salt packets and emptied them onto her wound. She hissed.

Not enough.

He jumped up and ran to the kitchen. Cabinet doors were flung open, the contents sifted through. He ignored what fell to the floor, interested in only the one ingredient.

"Come on, Tika. Every proper shifter has a ton of salt." The only thing that can offset silver toxicity should never be in short supply.

Finally! He gathered the container and a cup he filled with water. As he ran back to Tika, he poured salt into the water. Not ideal, but if she hadn't been shanked with a big dose, home brew saline was best.

She teetered on consciousness and her hand had fallen limp to her side, revealing a gaping wound. He overturned the contents of the glass directly on it. Tika moaned in pain, but was too weak to fight against it.

Nothing more could be done for her and there was more to take care of.

The two intruders hadn't yet healed. The one with a knife sticking out of his heart wouldn't begin healing until it was out, the blade suspending in him stasis. Handy. Chayton would wait to remove it. Odds were fifty-fifty for the guy with a hole in his head. Sometimes recovery was fast.

Instead of securing them with cuffs, he plunged a knife into the second shifter's heart. He'd pull them out when he had time to interrogate them.

He squatted on his heels and rubbed a hand over his scalp stubble. He had a few calls to make while waiting.

***

Kaitlyn sank to the bed. It was where she slept the second night while Waylon took the couch. Of course, he'd heard the full phone call with Chayton and understood everything.

"Want to talk?" He'd been giving her sidelong glances, like he was dying to ask, but she hadn't said much of anything since the call yesterday.

She scoffed. "He didn't want me. Enough said."

Waylon folded his arm, his biceps bulging. He was a prime specimen she knew nothing about. His place had an open layout, because it was in a warehouse. A punching bag that'd seen better days hung from the rafters. She knew how it felt. Especially after she went twenty rounds with it last night once she found out the roads were still blocked with snow.

"Chayton Eagle is your mate."

She nodded, her gaze on the floor. "He swore himself to someone else and is honoring that vow."

Waylon's scent swelled with anger and surprise. "What an idiot."

"Yeah."

"Want to fuck?"

She scowled at him, but a smile played at her lips at his playful tone.

He broke into a smile. "I get it. Friend-zoned. Let's go get some lunch before you take off."

Why couldn't he have been her mate? He looked out for everyone, a real friend when she was in need.

Why did she need a mate?

"I need to go, but thanks for the offer. And don't let anyone tell you you're not awesome." She gathered her items and headed for the door. "I mean it. Thank you."

"Anything." His answering smile held a hint of regret in his eyes.

Kaitlyn loaded her gear into the SUV. The rumble of larger engines crisscrossing town echoed in the distance. The plows continued clearing the roads. She hoped they attacked the back roads to the lodge. They'd never find all the roads, but her pack took care of those.

The drive back to the lodge was uneventful, much to her disappointment. Something to take her mind off her emotional woes would've been appreciated.

Chayton had been so jealous. Chalk it up to all the other idiosyncrasies she'd experienced from him. Like going from insulting and derisive to caring and territorial.

No, she couldn't dwell on it. It encouraged memories of them in the woods when he'd been so worried about her well-being.

Activity around the lodge was minimal. She parked in the large garage and trudged to her cabin.

God, it felt good to be home.

And lonely.

She dumped her gear and started the process of sorting and cataloguing inventory. She'd lost some weapons and her ammo supply was down. Those would need to be reported and replaced.

Footsteps on her porch gave her pause. She didn't feel like talking, to anyone. Her time with her sister and Waylon was what she'd needed. Facing others now held no appeal. Not even Cassie. But she had to face her team someday and they might have questions.

She answered the soft tap at the door. Commander Fitzsimmons stood on the landing. His expression was carefully neutral, but she sensed an *I don't want to have this talk* mood from him.

"Tell me what's going on." Ever to the point, the commander brokered no sway in his order. Since she'd already reported their mission to him, he was asking about the rest.

"Commander, I owe you my life, but this is really personal. I promise it won't affect my work."

He cocked his head at her and shoved his hands in his pockets. If it was a casual stance meant to put her at ease, it didn't work. Her boss didn't do casual.

"If Jace had been injured on a mission, would you have left him at the colony, during a snowstorm?"

Touché. "Cassie would kill me if I did." And Jace wouldn't have been in another female's bed.

"Cut the shit, Kaitlyn."

Defeat. She spilled everything while she stood in the doorway and the commander remained planted on her deck. He didn't move, his expression didn't twitch. He assessed her and her words. It was disconcerting, but made the telling easier. The story rushed out and when she was done, she leaned against the doorway, waiting for his reaction.

"I need you to go back."

"No way." She'd rather go back to being an aimless human than find Chayton.

"This was your mission and it isn't done yet." He stared hard at her. "The rogues you hunted weren't typical and they were getting help from packs in the colony."

"Mato can take care of it. We don't need to step in."

"You do when they attack a Guardian to get to Mato's daughter. There's something else going on and you would've figured it out if you'd stayed and followed up."

"Tika was attacked?"

"By three men who intended to kill her." He stalled and she knew she wouldn't like the rest. "Chayton was there, fought them off, and saved her."

Chayton was there...

"Has he questioned them yet?"

"No, Tika's life came first. You need to go back and finish the mission. You and Chayton let this dispute between you interfere with sorting out the real issues that led to the rogues terrorizing the entire county. And you and Chayton need to settle this shit. I can't have you ignoring each other and refusing to work together."

Exactly what she didn't want to do. The bottom of the lake was looking really good right now.

"I thought he'd stay there to live and work. Mato's tagged him as the next leader." Would he bring Tika back with him as long as Mato was still in position?

"Mato might think he's doing the best for his colony and his family, but the shifter world doesn't work that way anymore. Rogues and traitors indicate more than an issue with the colony members. It points to high dissatisfaction with Mato and his leadership that shifters are willing to give their lives to stop him."

No choice but to accept what her boss was saying. She'd fucked up, hadn't looked past her drama with Chayton. "When do you want me to go back?"

"Now." He turned to go.

She closed the door after he left and faced her gear. Time to pack it all back up.

Think like a Guardian. Chayton would need his gear replenished.

Taking a few moments to gather her things, she made a stop at Chayton's cabin.

His door wasn't locked. She'd never been in there. Had any of the others?

She stepped in. It was…nice. Expecting plain furnishings and empty walls, she stared. Beaded artwork was hung with pride. Blankets draped over the chairs had colorful—were those porcupine quills sewn in? After picking those out of her hide following an unfortunate encounter with the prickly rodent, she couldn't imagine turning them into her hobby.

It struck her how homey the cabin felt. Not only did his home express a whole different side to him, but it was comfortable as well.

His bedroom was no different. In fact, she could curl up on his bed and sleep like Goldilocks. Or gaze in awe at the painted buffalo hide draped across his mattress.

She ran her hands over the smooth surface. The pictures were stories. The birth of a son, a young boy dancing during a ceremony, a young man going off on his own. She wondered if they were of his life. Then she got to the one with flames. The fire his mother died in?

A tear rolled down her cheek. This hide was more than a symbol of his history; it was everything he shared with his mother, his ina. Spirit Moon was one of the few places where he could closely connect with his heritage.

Perhaps she'd forgive him one day.

Chapter Fourteen

"You're safe here with your parents." Chayton evaluated Tika's curled-up form on the chair. "My *ahte's* watching outside."

Tika nodded woodenly. She hadn't spoken much since she'd come to in her mother's arms. He'd had to physically restrain Mato from beheading the two survivors secured in Tika's house.

He stuffed his hands into his pockets. Tika wasn't who he wanted to mate, but he didn't like seeing a young innocent so shaken. Violence happened to all shifters, though, whether or not they lived long enough. Plans streamed through his mind. He'd get the names from Mato, interrogate them—not that they'd talk—and at least glean any clues he could of their pack affiliation and personal habits.

A chill shivered across his scalp. He brushed a hand over it, used to the sensation, but this was different.

Something was off. He wandered to the window in time to see Mato streaking across the yard as a wolf.

That son of a bitch.

Without a word, Chayton stormed down the stairs where he passed Zitkana, wearing a defensive, righteous expression. He burst out of the house and charged after Mato.

He wouldn't make it in time. Mato as a wolf would make better time and the silver glinting from his mouth said he went armed. Mato would get to Tika's, shift, and execute.

Chayton jumped fences and plowed through snow piles until he reached the little house at the end of the block.

Slamming through the door, he almost ran into a nude Mato holding a machete.

Skidding to stop, his heart pounding, ready to tackle someone, Chayton looked around. What was the guy standing there for?

No bodies.

"*Shit.*" He knew the shifters couldn't escape, but he didn't expect someone to take them. Cursing his lack of foresight, he went to shove a hand through his hair only to hit stubble, which spiked his irritation.

"You should've put someone on guard." Mato's lilting tone grew more pronounced with his anger.

"Who? Who can you fucking trust in this colony? I was watching out for your daughter, you wouldn't leave her side, *Ahte* is guarding your house. *Who is left?*"

A muscle danced in Mato's cheek. Damn right. Mato should be able to rattle off a long list of trustworthy shifters that encompassed ninety-nine point five percent of his colony. But throw in the trust factor and he couldn't name one. Chayon had suggested Trevon, but Mato had brushed him off, too. Control freak.

"Come on." Chayton took one last look, hoping they'd dropped a knife or something to give him the advantage for once. Was a stray wallet or family photo too much to hope for? At least he knew their faces. He could work with that. "We're going back to your place for a nice long talk."

***

"Dammit, Mato!" Chayton slammed his palms on top of the table in Mato's conference room. "You can't round up the town for interrogation."

Mato leaned over the table, jabbing his index finger on the surface. "It's my town and they attacked my daughter. I will damn well do what I please. I'd think you'd be beside me. You were the one who had to save your own mate."

Exactly. He couldn't help but keep comparing Tika with Kaitlyn. If the intruders had gotten close enough to hit Kaitlyn, she would've either had a salt packet on her or made it to the kitchen and saved herself.

Chayton steadied his voice to get his point across. "You doing what you want is what started all of this. Did you kick those shifters out? Is that why they went rogue? You cut them off when they spoke against you."

A beet-red flush took over Mato's face. Bingo.

"I dedicated my life to this community and what happened? Two children murdered." Mato sat back down and shook his head. "We waited damn near a century for another child. They weren't getting Tika. I knew if I tied her to you, no one would cross a Guardian. You could fight and none of their abilities would work on you."

That's why Chayton was chosen, his future disregarded, to secure one for Tika. He released a long breath and counted to ten. He knew he'd been manipulated and hearing the depth of it didn't help. It wasn't coincidence they caught him after the vulnerable time of his *ina's* death and he'd caved; they'd hunted him.

Chayton hadn't been around when Mato's young kids were killed. His position as a Guardian had carried him away from home barely out of his teens, but he'd come back in an official capacity to investigate the incident—after Mato had "dealt" with it. "The deaths of your first children may not have been targeted assassinations."

"Bullshit," Zitkana announced from the doorway, her expression severe, unyielding. "Everyone knew where they played and who with. Silver didn't accidentally lace their toys."

"Too bad I couldn't investigate." There'd been no one left. Mato had executed the family the toys belonged to, whose own kids had also been victims. Chayton rose and eyed both Zitkana and Mato. "Now I will investigate and you two will stay out of my way." Zitkana opened her mouth to argue, but he held up a hand and continued. "You will do this because I'm a Guardian and the one you trusted with your daughter."

A honeysuckle scent wrapped around him, one he should've noticed if he weren't so emotionally charged.

Mato and Zitkana both turned to peer out of the room, into the hallway where Kaitlyn stood, having heard Chayton's last statement.

His body rejoiced at her proximity, his head cursed it. Why did the commander send her back here?

Mato made a disgusted noise. "Guardian."

"We'll start by looking through your records. Everything you have, we'll sift through it all." She exuded professionalism even though she had to be seething inside to have to be close to him, helping to find who hurt Tika. "I understand how close this is to you. We'll give you regular updates, but any punishment will need to be doled out by us."

Zitkana's glare could've cut a swath a mile wide through the forest. "Find them, make them pay." She shoved past Kaitlyn. "Or I will."

Kaitlyn ignored Chayton, her neutral expression on Mato. "The records."

Chapter Fifteen

What seventh hell was this? Working in close proximity with Kaitlyn, while hints of Waylon lingered on her, was a torture Chayton could only wish on his worst enemies. His blood pressure had to be sky-high.

She studiously ignored his pointed glares, only saying, "We can't let more drama interfere with this mission."

Chayton noticed her subtle use of *more* drama instead of *our* drama. She'd written him off.

"We still need to talk," he growled.

She glanced up to him, then to the closed door. "And do you think this is a good place for it?"

A breach in her expression revealed deep hurt. He'd caused it.

He took a stack of records and pushed them toward her. "Why don't you look through these and I'll take the laptop. I know what they look like and can spot them in any photos."

The gentleness of his tone must've surprised her. It didn't assuage the effect of his actions, but he didn't want to add to it. She swiveled the computer toward him, the action stirring up her scent.

"How was Waylon?" He was a dog with a bone, what could he say?

"Fine." She ruffled through the papers, but he could tell she'd lost her focus. "And Tika?"

"Recovered, but in shock." *Weak.*

"Good thing you were there, then." She readjusted her pencil and notepad and focused on the documents. Her emotions shut down as if she decided to pretend he wasn't in the room.

It was for the best. He scanned the computer through news clippings and logged in to social media to try to find an image of one of the attackers.

Hours of research later, he pushed back, frustrated and hungry. The sun had set long ago and would rise in only a few more.

"Enough." He cleared his browsing history. "We need food and rest. I'm sure there's an empty room in this monstrosity for you to catch some Zs in."

"There's a little motel down the road. I'll stay there."

After working next to her half the night, he didn't want her to leave. "I wouldn't put it past whoever's behind this to target you if you're alone."

She rammed the papers into the filing cabinet. "I'm not staying here with you and Tika."

Full of resentment. He didn't blame her. It hadn't dawned on him where he'd sleep.

"I'll take the floor in the conference room." It was a good enough compromise. One that would keep her here.

She sighed and hefted her backpack. "Fine. I just want to be up shortly after sunrise to search Tika's home."

"Good idea. You might see something I missed. I won't bother Zitkana. There's a guest room on the second floor—" Right across from the room Tika was in. "Actually, the den might be better. It's around the corner." *And closer to me.*

***

Kaitlyn stretched out on the couch in the den. For once her mind wasn't on Chayton but on the details she'd unearthed during her research.

Execution records, notes from town meetings, population rises and falls. Mostly falls. Geez, the whole town could be suspects. No wonder Chayton was such a dick—he was raised here.

Odd, because she liked Des, but centuries could've mellowed the guy out. Not to mention she sensed a similar instability in him that she did in her own dad.

She'd spotted Cian running in the trees as she drove past Valley Moon. How'd he always sensed she was near?

Her eyelids drifted closed. Dawn would arrive shortly and she needed rest. This mission was emotionally and physically brutal, and it'd end sooner if she kept her wits intact. She tediously kept her thoughts off Chayton, thinking about Cian, her sister, anything.

The heavy veil of sleep hung over her, muscles loosened, her breathing steadied. Ultimate relaxation allowed the image to form of a bald male with flashing brown eyes. He kneeled next to her, his broad shoulders blocking out the rest of the dark room. He felt so real, as if he was really there.

At last. She wanted him closer. Nothing would be right until he was closer.

"Kaitlyn," he whispered. He stroked his calloused fingertips along her jaw.

A tremor sizzled down her spine. Her body had craved him like ice cream on a sweltering summer day. She ran her hands along his bare shoulders, up to his head, and pulled him closer. His returning hair teased her skin, sending shock waves from her fingertips to her toes.

Skin-on-skin was the only thing that could satisfy her need. She sat up, and while he watched, she peeled her shirt off. Next went her bra. She cursed staying dressed before she went to sleep.

His eyes glittered in the dark. Kaitlyn sensed his impatience before he lowered his head past her lips, down to her breasts. Warm lips closed around one nipple. With one of his arms wrapped under her, she reclined to enjoy the feeling. His tongue flicked against her sensitive flesh. She arched into him, sighed when he unsnapped her pants with his other hand.

Yesss. Her legs spread of their own accord, as much as they could in her pants. When his fingers hit her clit, she almost shouted, but he released her nipple and pressed his lips against hers.

She *had* to taste him. She licked across the seam of his lips and he opened readily for her. Ahhh, there was his savory flavor. All male.

Her hips undulated against his hand; his fingers played with her. Strung her up, stretched out her pleasure. She whimpered, but withheld a moan. Her rational mind warned her she was still in the den and to not make a lot of noise.

She twined her arms around him, the low rumble in his chest vibrated against her hands. Combined with the magic his fingers created, her climax hit. Her nails scored his back with the effort of holding her scream in. She shuddered and rocked, he held her to him, his mouth catching any sound she made.

Her breath came out in pants and she broke contact with his lips. His hand stayed at her core, their eyes locked. His were filled with male satisfaction, regret, and longing. She stroked a hand down his cheek. He opened his mouth to speak—

Her eyes flew open. She looked down at her bare breasts and her undone pants. Her gaze darted around the room. *It was a dream. It was a dream.*

She snatched her shirt and bra from where she dropped them in her sleep and dressed. How had she undressed without waking? Dissipating heat lingered at her sex. She'd orgasmed for real. It'd all been so tangible—his touch, his taste, him.

Being plagued with dreams like that might very well drive her feral.

Chapter Sixteen

Chayton stared at the ceiling. Soft morning light brightened the room, but he wasn't going to move until he heard Kaitlyn was awake.

Fuck…that dream. No sleep since he'd woken from it. No one could sleep through an erection that hard. He'd sought no relief, every breath exquisite pain. It hadn't died down and he needed it to before anyone else in the household was up. On this, he hoped Kaitlyn ignored him when they met up.

His thoughts drifted back to the score marks he felt on his back. How the hell…

It was a dream. An amazing, wish it was real, dream. The real thing would've been eight thousand times better. And he would've finished—over and over again.

With a stifled groan, he rolled off his back to a sitting position. The floor of the conference room was adequate enough, he'd slept in worse places. He massaged his neck muscles while waiting for the laptop to boot up. Hours ago, he'd gone through online records, news articles of the colony. Spirit Moon embraced technology in a way that kept them more isolated.

He was tired of scouring pictures and decided to log onto the "othernet" concealed and run by their kind. Searching a few choice phrases pulled up nothing obvious like rebellion, and he had plenty to sift through.

A soft knock on the door and Kaitlyn entered.

Great, his erection had almost faded. His gaze flicked up to her and crashed back to his screen. How did she get more beautiful every day—in the same clothes, with the same hairstyle?

"How was the couch?" He shouldn't have asked. Images of his dream dominated. With great effort, he reined in his lust before it overwhelmed the room.

Mothballs. Week-old garbage. Clogged toilets. All barely strong enough to blanket his thoughts. Especially once the stain of a blush tinted her cheeks and her gaze darted away.

Was it possible she had the same dream? They were mates.

No, he mentally shook his head. It did neither one of them any good to follow up.

She dropped her armload of papers on the tabletop and ignored his question. "I decided to take a different route in this investigation."

"Same here, but if there's anything on Spirit Moon in our underground web, then it's hidden well."

She sat down and spread the papers out in front of her. "I decided to check into the deaths of Mato's children. There isn't much for records, which is understandable. It was a brave shifter who put all that on paper after Mato killed everyone involved."

"Back in the old days, his pack and clan members acted as his staff. You're right, he would've been too distraught to record any of it."

"Not much at all is recorded. But I went looking for anything on the other family."

Chayton stood and pulled up a chair next to her. "The parents Mato executed."

She bobbed her head while her keen expression picked out details on the documents. "Most people assumed they were innocent. After all, they lost their own children, but there's two other lines of thought."

He was in the group who'd assumed they were innocent and Mato had reacted rashly, not that anyone blamed him.

Kaitlyn kept her voice low to prevent eavesdropping. "I wouldn't put it past some shifters to sacrifice their own, but I don't think that was the case, so I ruled it out. An accident is highly unlikely. Not impossible, but a shifter family with little kids won't keep random silver around the house. But what if they had friends or family who knew their kids were good friends with Mato's?"

"It was a different time, why don't you think kids cutting themselves while playing could've been an accident?"

She let out a laugh. "A different time, no shit. The kids were playing house—with real cutlery. But that's the thing. I'm sure they did it all the time. If it was like my aunt and uncle's place, who fostered all different ages, any of their old shit turned into toys. You tell me, old man, who controlled the colony's silver supply at the time?"

His lips twitched. Old man. He was only two centuries older than her. "No different than today. Anyone can have it if they can get their hands on it, but it has to be registered with the leader."

"So then why didn't Mato go berserk and kill anyone who had silver under their roof?"

He stared at her. "It would've been too many people."

Her eyes bright, she spun a document toward him. "Or he trusted them implicitly."

The names on the paper were all familiar to him. Shifters who might not be a member of the clan his own meager pack was in, but in one of the other clans that comprised the colony.

He frowned. "What am I supposed to be seeing here? Many of these are Mato's own pack members." Made sense Mato would predominantly trust his own.

Her sly smile was the sexiest he'd ever seen. "Their occupations."

Woodcutters, recorder, teachers, repairmen.

"Okay?" Color him stupid, he couldn't see what she was getting at.

"Now look at this."

Another document slid in front of him. Yellowed with age, he would've dismissed it. A hundred years is a long time to hold on to maintenance forms.

"It's a bill for services rendered to patch a roof after a bad storm." His attention caught on the name of the repairman from Mato's pack. He sank back into his chair, stunned. "For the roof of the family Mato suspected of killing his kids." And the name of the repairman was also listed on the silver form.

"But the rogues haven't been from his pack, or even his own clan, right?"

He nodded, wondering the same thing.

"What if the goal is to put this shifter, the repairman, in a place of power? What if they've been undermining Mato all these years and encouraging rogues to wreak havoc to weaken Mato's hold on the colony?"

If he could, he'd drag her onto his lap and kiss her senseless. Too bad solving this case wouldn't solve their problem. "Then they wouldn't use anyone from Mato's inner circle. Use shifters from packs known to cause trouble, throw off the scent, unsettle Mato's power."

She tapped the name. "We start there."

The conference door swung open, with Mato guarding the doorway. "Start where?"

Another scent wafted in and Chayton wanted to curse. Tika squeezed past her dad, still looking wan and frail. In a hearty shifter, recovering from silver toxicity was a long road. Too bad Mato had unintentionally kept her weak.

"Good morning." Tika glanced back and forth between him and Kaitlyn. "Chay, do you want to grab something to eat."

Kaitlyn's gaze pinned the table as she gathered up contracts and records.

"No, we need to get started," he said, softy. He'd been a fool to make the vow, an even bigger fool to not entertain the notion of how it would've hurt his future mate.

"Where are you going?" Mato fisted his hands at his side. As if Chayton would be idiotic enough to tell him. Mato would tear through his pack members, decimate his clan, and *maybe* ask questions later.

"Tika," Zitkana called from down the hall, "let the Guardians work. Come get some food."

The girl looked like she was going to shuffle to Chayton to kiss him, but he stumbled out of his chair to retrieve his laptop, holding it like a shield. He busied himself putting it away and packing his gear.

Uncertainly crossed Tika's features and it wasn't about whether she should go eat breakfast. She left the room.

Chayton suppressed a sigh of relief and spoke to Mato. "We'll brief you when we're done."

"The hell you will. I demand to be updated."

"It's a hunch, that's all." Kaitlyn pushed back from the table and held her hand out for Chayton's pack. When he handed it over, she stuffed all the papers in it. He almost choked at her audacity in front of Mato.

So did Mato. His eyes flashed. "Those are my property."

"They are part of an official Guardian investigation." His partner knew better. As soon as they left, Mato would've locked himself up with them until he found what they had. The male advanced on Kaitlyn.

Chayton stepped between them. She could handle herself, but she'd embarrass the shit out of Mato and they had enough hurdles to cross. "You acted impulsively before and likely executed an innocent family. If you do it again and we're wrong, then you're doing nothing but proving this little rebellion right, that you're unfit to lead."

"I dedicate my entire life to this colony. *I lost children for it*." Mato shook with contained rage.

For that, Chayton was truly sorry. And sorry that Mato had ruled with such single-mindedness it'd opened his family up to being targets.

Kaitlyn slung the pack over her shoulder. "If you don't want to lose more, you'll let us do our jobs."

***

Kaitlyn studied the terrain as it flew by. Chayton wove through the mountain roads, wasting time and throwing any nosey shifters off their trail. She'd seen a familiar flash of white.

"I'm just saying, I can't believe you said that." Chayton's smile was too distracting, she had to keep her focus out her window.

"It worked, didn't it. And it's true." Kaitlyn despised Tika with every fiber of her being, but her Guardian instincts wouldn't allow the weak to suffer. "She shouldn't be such a pussy." That was true, too.

He snorted, then sobered. "I swear she stood there and let herself get shanked."

"I guess you'll have to teach her to fight." Ugh. Damn her heart of melted butter. The girl would be even more of a target with Chayton. Why couldn't Kaitlyn be a bitch and be wickedly delighted Tika was a walking target?

He didn't say anything, and really, what was there to say?

"Look." Her gruff voice made her wince. "Waylon's nothing more than a friend now. I know I have to move on someday while you… But I'm not jumping into anything with anyone."

She wasn't so desperate for a mate that she needed fill the void with another dude or two.

How many partners would she have to be with to be as satisfied as Chayton had made her?

Not enough, but she'd deal later.

His profile was grim, his knuckles white on the wheel. "I'm sorry. I really am. I was two centuries old, been all over the country, with no hint of a mate. I just thought…" His expression softened and filled with regret. "Zitkana was so damn persistent about how I could protect her daughter. I never thought she'd not teach Tika to protect herself."

Kaitlyn couldn't think of anything to say that wouldn't spike her anger. She stared out the window. They were approaching town.

"For the record, I haven't done anything with her, either. Not since I met you. Except the peck she gave me when we first arrived."

Her anger remained a slow boil that would always be there and she needed to accept it. "Why a blood oath?"

He rolled a heavy shoulder. "I think my ability to absorb others' abilities clinched it. Tika can slow motions, but like her, it isn't very strong."

At least the girl had a power. Not many missions made Kaitlyn feel like an entire failure as this one had.

"What's wrong?" Chayton asked.

"Nothing."

Chayton side-eyed her. "Is it the ability thing?"

She sucked in her lower lip. They'd reached a middle ground where they could be civil to each other. She didn't want to return to his cutting remarks on her lack of ability.

He tapped his fingers on the wheel. "How do others' mental powers affect you?"

Kaitlyn continued chewing her lower lip. "None have really been used on me."

"Not true. *Ahte* said he tried to read you. Mato surely tried to control you. You negate power."

"No," she scoffed. But…a little excitement started to build.

"Kaitlyn," his voice dropped low, "*Ahte* said he's only met one other shifter who has that ability. Cian."

Kaitlyn stared at him. "You know he's my dad?"

"You know he's your dad?"

"He told me after he saved me from the lake."

"Huh." Chayton rubbed his chin. "My guess is your growing stronger the more you're in the shifter world."

"Huh," she echoed. She'd think on it later, have a blast getting the guys to test their abilities on her. "Are you heading to the hardware store?"

"The whole colony knows our vehicle, so we can't do a stakeout without Mato finding out who we're watching. The male we're after was the one Mato was arguing with when we first arrived."

"Thomas." Oh, did she remember. "We should have an excuse to go inside. What do we have that's broken?"

Chayton thought for a minute. "Nothing has to be broken. I'll keep 'em busy. You wander around and browse."

"As in snoop? Eagle, you know me so well."

He grunted his response and fell quiet. Maybe they'd reach a non-awkward stage someday.

Chapter Seventeen

The store came into view. It was a good-sized warehouse on the edge of town. From the organized piles of lumber in the back, it wasn't just tools they sold. There'd be more workers than two or three. Chayton better walk in and be a diva to give Kaitlyn time to casually make her rounds.

He parked and they sauntered in. Chayton had grabbed a pouch out of his pack. She'd seen it before, one of his leather-working projects. They entered the place and Kaitlyn was struck by how normal it was, a sensation that had never died when she dealt with contemporary colonies.

Work clothes and some styles with a western flare hung in racks off to her right. Several aisles of tools filled most of the store and the homey scent of fresh wood grew stronger the farther they got inside.

"Chayton Eagle, you are in big trouble, young man."

Kaitlyn turned toward the maternal voice.

Chayton did the same, but he wore a broad smile. "Auntie," he greeted warmly.

A female slightly shorter than Kaitlyn approached. Her gray-streaked black hair was wrapped in a bun. She wore the standard blue apron indicating she worked in the store.

The female wrapped Chayton in a bear hug. "I heard talk you were in town, but couldn't believe you wouldn't stop in to see me."

Kaitlyn blinked at the pair. He was the most at ease as she'd ever seen him. A smile ready on his lips, his tone filled with love and respect.

He beckoned to Kaitlyn, his eyes dancing with delight. "Savoy, this is Shilo. She's a part of my pack. I call her my auntie, but we're not blood relatives. Auntie, this is my partner, Kaitlyn."

Shilo nodded toward Kaitlyn. "His *ina* and I grew up together." She turned back to Chayton. "I still check on Des, make sure he's ornery as ever. I'd love to think you came here to see me, but I think my heart would break."

Chayton chuckled. "I would've before I left, Auntie." He held up his project. "I'm almost done with this waist pouch. It needs a ring for the strap. What do you stock here?"

Shilo took Chayton's bag and examined it with a critical eye. "Looks solid. Your skills haven't faded at all."

Kaitlyn took advantage of the moment. "It's been forever since I've indulged in retail therapy. You two catch up while I wander around."

She broke and chose the clothing first to look more natural. She ran her hands over the heavy-duty material and jeans meant for more than showing off her ass. No employees approached her. She'd have to go in search of them.

The next section was boots and shoes. Sturdy, like the clothing. Score. A guy stocking shoeboxes. He glanced up at her, surprise registering. She guessed because she was a stranger. A friendly greeting and she moved on.

Not Thomas.

There was a group of three lean, young male employees chatting several aisles away. They were casually standing with hands in pockets, or leaning on shelving. As she drifted closer, they grew quiet.

"Can I help you with something?" The male who spoke already faced her. His tone said *get the fuck out*.

I'm getting warmer. "I'm just browsing while Chayton finds what he needs."

The other two males turned and a cloud of hostility bloomed. None of them were Thomas, but she'd bet they worked for him in more than just the store.

She pasted on a friendly smile. "I'm surprised by the amenities offered in this place. I don't see a comprehensive setup like this in many colonies. It's usually just a shop on Main Street."

They stared at her. She suspected they communicated among each other.

The one who spoke to her originally narrowed his eyes. "What's Chayton looking for?"

She waved her hand nonchalantly. "Something for a satchel he made. Impressive work." She snickered. "No way I could do that. My Home Ec teacher flat out told me I was a lost cause." No reaction. "I'll let you get back to work. I don't get to shop much anymore so I'll take it while I can."

Wandering away, the space between her shoulders itched. If their glares were silver-laced daggers, she'd be squealing on the floor.

Three males seemed suspicious about what you were here for. None of them Thomas. Same pack, perhaps?

I've passed two more employees. None of them him, either. There can't be that many more workers on shift.

The lumberyard? There wasn't much of the store she hadn't wandered.

It'd be too obvious if we went there.

Obvious, or probable cause? Not to sound conceited, but the only time I get that hostile reaction from a dude is when I'm about to go Guardian on his ass. Those three are up to something and they don't want us around.

She rounded an end cap of the aisle. Chayton was squatting and hefting various metal rings, all slightly bigger than the one on her favorite tote. His stark features while meticulously choosing a ring for his project opened a yawning pit deep inside her. At first, she'd only known him as proud and pompous. She'd seen him at his worst and still fell for him. What the hell was she going to do after witnessing him carefully choosing a ring for his leather-working hobby, dressed as a combat action figure, his face relaxed after catching up with a loved one? She feared after seeing the real Chayton that moving on was futile.

He frowned and rose. "Where's my auntie?"

They both pivoted to look around. Only the lingering scent of Shilo was found.

His dark eyes grew concerned. "She said she'd be right back after clocking out for break so we could chat."

He inched his hand up to his hip where his gun was holstered.

The general atmosphere in the store grew dimmer. The lights were on, the sky was clear, but something was coming for them.

She pulled her gun and held it pointing downward, but she was tensed and ready to use it.

They both crept to the end of the aisle, Kaitlyn facing forward, Chayton at her back, covering her from behind. She crested the shelving in time to see a shadow dart away. She cleared each direction and they edged out in the same position, working in harmony like a dance.

Two steps and she peeked around the next set of shelving in time to see a menagerie of items thrown at her. A cacophonous clang of metal showered around them. She ducked back, screws and nails clattering past.

Chayton cursed. *Can you keep advancing?*

There's a door to the back of the building twenty feet away.

Kaitlyn sensed another presence behind them, a change in the air. She trusted Chayton to have eyes on it.

During her calm but swift forward momentum, she caught sight of a male jumping on top of a shelving set. He tipped it into the next one to create a domino effect. Heavy shelving groaned, intermixed with screeches of metal on metal. The entire monstrosity toppled against the next set.

More crashes from the other end of the store, and yard utensils flew into their path from the falling units. Each end cap they cleared, shadows darted.

They're herding us toward the back, Chayton said, and yeah, she'd come to the same conclusion.

The familiar rush of adrenaline lined her blood vessels. Most people would be scared, most shifters, too, but her Guardian blood thrived on this.

Finally, we can get this over with.

He snorted behind her, probably thought the same damn thing.

I've got your five, he warned before he shot.

A male yelped. She smirked. They approached the back door. As she was pivoting to go through, she anticipated a reaction from their tormentors. They'd been predictable in their efforts, flitting back and forth, only the three of them.

She paused for a heartbeat to let one cross at the other end of the aisle. Chayton stalled, too, and waited for her to take the shot.

As soon as she detected movement, she squeezed off a round. She knew she'd hit her target before the shout of pain.

Chayton stuck close as they flowed through the door to a massive section of the warehouse. A giant overhead door was open at one end leading to the lumberyard.

I guess we get to see all their wood. Her words lacked humor.

I will burn it all if they hurt Auntie. Do you have the bullets we can kill these fuckers with?

Not enough. I loaded our backups with the silver. Too bad they couldn't use them solely for ammo, but it was too risky. They might plug someone who didn't earn the silver injection, or their own weapon could get used against them. If these were the shifters they were after, and they probably were, it was highly likely these shifters carried their own silver stash.

With Chayton a wall at her back, she started forward progress to the lumberyard. The faint scent of Shilo was laced with fury and fear. Kaitlyn was the first to admit she was relieved—both because the female was still alive and because she wasn't in on the conspiracy.

The rumble of a growl came from Chayton. He scented it, too.

Kaitlyn tasted the air, inhaling deeply. It was difficult to determine the number. Everyone who'd worked today tainted the area, but she narrowed her focus to any scents involving deception.

The three males that were herding them, plus two more and two females.

Seven to two. Three if Shilo wasn't incapacitated.

Meh. She'd had worse odds before. Cataloguing her weapons where they pressed against her body, she mentally fortified herself. There'd be little space for thought. Once the fighting started, it'd be all instinct and reflex. The moments leading up to the battle were where some people disintegrated.

They approached the gaping opening. The pathway toward it was lined with pallets of sheetrock and lumber. Outside, even more pallets were stacked with mason blocks and landscaping material. Little movement could be detected. No birds flew overhead, no sounds of nature could be heard. Every living thing sensed the impending fight.

Ready, Cinnamon?

She suppressed her chuckle. *Let's take 'em down, Eagle.*

Across the yard from the opening of the door were stacks of bricks several feet high. Her keen eyesight detected a shifter hiding between the shelving. In less than a second, she raised her gun, aimed, and squeezed. The shifter jerked and snarled.

A scuffle sounded behind her. Chayton fired his gun and swore.

I'm switching to silver. This is ridiculous. They're going to keep coming like Day of the Dead.

He covered her while she shoved the gun with regular bullets back in its holster and withdrew the one loaded with silver-washed bullets. She did the same for him. Both locked and loaded with shifter-fatal ammo.

Taking the turn into the lumberyard, she tensed. Was it going to be an old-fashioned gunfight like the movies her dad used to watch?

She crouched to become a smaller mark.

Lunging to the side, she assessed the scene past the stack of two-by-fours bordering the doors.

Shilo lay on the concrete, a dark-haired shifter crouched above her with a handsaw. Kaitlyn took the shot.

She nailed him in the chest, but more rounds rained down on her. She jerked back into the warehouse, Chayton moving with her.

Your aunt's knocked out, but they were ready to decapitate her.

An unfamiliar whirring noise and scrape of tires on asphalt drowned out any other sound.

Kaitlyn edged out to peek. *They're charging us with a forklift.* She aimed, but didn't want to waste the precious ammo.

Chayton was firing at attackers behind her, so she bided her time.

The forklift approached. At least two shifters used it for cover, not counting the one driving.

Kaitlyn shoved her gun in its holder and pulled out a knife for each hand.

Slivers exploded near her head. The woodpile shuddered. She ignored it and prepared to jump. The blades of the forklift cleared her hiding spot. She leaped onto the blades and rolled to the other side. It exposed her. Bullets hit metal and asphalt, but her moving form was too difficult to hit. The forklift driver stopped, but she'd already cleared the back and kicked at one of the shifters. The shifter's gun clattered the ground.

Their shock registered as a rancid tang. She smashed her elbow into his nose. Before he recovered, she'd jammed her knee into his balls. Didn't matter the species, it was a target that worked every time. The second shifter was trying to circle around behind her. She stabbed with one of the knives, aiming to hit the first shifter's carotid. He batted it away. She ducked and jabbed him in the gut with her other knife. The blade lodged in his abdomen and she jerked it downward.

He screamed in pain and buckled to the ground. She spun on the second attacker. He raised a gun and she aimed a high kick at his hand. The gun fired at the sky. The forklift lurched forward. She jumped back. Grunts from Chayton told her he'd taken on the driver.

The shifter she'd gutted writhed on the asphalt. She jumped over him to a clear area to fight. Her second attacker bared his fangs and lunged.

Her grin was grim. If he thought to engage her in hand to hand, or that he'd have the advantage once he got her on the ground, he was an idiot.

He grabbed her and she dropped, taking him by surprise. She abandoned one knife to grip his wrist and twist until bones ground together and cracked. While he snarled and adjusted his hold to compensate for the pain, she threw him off to the side and rolled with him.

Her remaining blade flashed in the sun as it arced to bury in his heart. Reaching to grab the gun with the special bullets, she flinched when the forklift jumped again and kept going. It was enough to distract her. The shifter with Kaitlyn's knife buried in his belly wrapped a hand around her ankle and yanked. She allowed him to drag her, then seized the first chance to slam her other boot into him.

A gunshot echoed. Fire seared through her side, stealing her air. She searched for where the bullet came from. Agony spread through skin. An older female with jet black hair pulled into a ponytail and even blacker eyes strode toward her, a snarl on her lips, and gun raised to shoot again.

The hold on her ankle grew weaker. Kaitlyn extricated herself, fumbled for the gun at her hip, but couldn't free it before the second shot hit her.

She bellowed as unusually intense pain spread across her thigh. Normal gunshots hurt, but this was like every nerve ending was coated in molten iron.

Silver, she told Chayton.

Chayton grunted back to her. A body hit the ground next to the forklift, but her gaze was on the female, who raised her weapon to the cab.

Gunshots boomed on either side of Kaitlyn. She hoped it was Chayton shooting the female. She used the reprieve to rifle through the pouch in her belt.

Her breaths were coming in pants and she could barely see between the agony and silver toxicity clouding her vision. Finally, her fingers landed on a paper packet. The tremors in her hands made it hard to hold on to.

She brought it up to her mouth and tore the edge off with her teeth. Granules of salt hit her tongue, but it wouldn't be good enough.

With shaking hands, she upended the packet over the wound in her side.

A ragged yell burst out of her. Kaitlyn blinked away the burning and searing pain to see if Chayton had taken out the shooter.

The shifter was on the ground and sensed Chayton approaching. He raised his weapon and fired one shot into each male she'd tackled.

Kaitlyn wanted to protest from the pain when he lifted her and carried her between the pallets and the forklift for cover. He gently laid her down and squatted next to her to pull out another salt container. She'd packed several, hoarded the damn things, but worried that with the bullets still in her, it wouldn't be enough. Whether they were made with silver, or washed in it, they were inside of her releasing all the poisonous metal they contained.

Her jaw clenched and she arched as he emptied another packet into her thigh wound.

"We took out five," he said, probably more to distract her. "There's at least two more."

"Sh-Sh-Shilo?" Her full body tremors weren't decreasing. Not a good sign.

"Alive." A male shouted from the direction of her prone form. "For now. Guardian, leave the female and come face me. You don't get to march into this whenever you want and tell us how to run things."

***

Chayton's upper lip curled into a snarl. Thomas. Had to be. There was still another female at large.

"So hiding behind rogues and letting them get killed for your dirty work is how it should go?" With steady movements, he withdrew the gun that was the deadlier one of the two from Kaitlyn's belt. She gazed up at him, her expression so full of suffering it could destroy him. But she was strong.

He pressed the gun into her hand. She blinked slow, probably didn't trust herself to try to nod. Her entire body visibly shook, her skin had lost much of its glow. That silver-laced lead had to be carved out of her as soon as possible.

He nodded in acknowledgment and spun to stalk away from the protection of the machinery.

A whistling noise had him lunging sideways as a knife embedded in the lumber on his right.

"That was a shit throw, Thomas." Chayton raised his gun as the shifter charged toward him. He squeezed off three rounds before the shifter was on him. Chayton was confident he'd plugged each bullet into him, but decades of rage fueled Thomas. Only real silver bullets would've been strong enough to fell him right away. Chayton's were only silver-washed.

He whipped his arms up in a defensive stance, bracing himself for bodily impact.

"You should've left after those rogues were killed." Thomas tackled Chayton before he could kick out.

They flew backward and the gun was bashed out of Chayton's hand, but he managed to remain upright.

"You should've challenged Mato like a real male." He curled forward to ram his elbows into Thomas's head. Blood seeped through the back of the male's shirt.

He should be dead any second.

Kaitlyn might be, too.

He sensed another female enter the lumberyard. Kaitlyn! Was she able to defend herself?

A gun fired, over and over again, until the clip was emptied. Which female was on the receiving end?

Thomas drew back to yank something out of the loop on his carpenter's jeans. A sharpening rod. He raised it to stab into Chayton, but his movements were hindered by the silver poisoning.

"Why don't you just die?" Chayton booted him under the chin.

Thomas arched backward and landed on his back, the metal rod fell from his fingers.

His mouth was moving. Chayton barely caught the words. "Mato isn't fit to lead. Tika is weak."

Chayton jumped to his feet. "You might be right, but we have traditions and laws for a reason."

Thomas coughed. Bloody spittle ran out of the corner of his mouth. "They will ruin your life like they ruined the colony."

What could Chayton say? They already had.

Thomas's fingers twitched and the metal rod hovered and flew to spear Chayton. In pure reflex, Chayton turned Thomas's telekinesis back on him. His own fingers twitched and the rod impaled Thomas's chest.

When the light left Thomas's eyes and he was good and dead, Chayton pivoted and ran to Kaitlyn. The stench of her poisoned blood was stronger than any of the deceased. He glanced over his shoulder at Shilo lying on the pavement. No blood marred her. She was even groaning and moving around.

Chayton scanned the area around Kaitlyn. So much blood. Sweet Mother, had the female shifter emptied her gun into Kaitlyn? Even if the bullets weren't silver, she wouldn't survive the onslaught with her other injuries.

He swept the area until a new set of boots caught his eye. They were sideways, the rest of the body stretched across the opening of the garage door. The female had come through and rounded on Kaitlyn, who'd filled her full of silver-lined holes.

His mate was amazing.

As he jogged to Kaitlyn, she searched through her pouch to withdraw a salt packet, then ripped it open with clattering teeth and dumped it on her wound. Repeat.

At least ten wrappers were scattered around her.

What a female.

He skidded onto his knees next to her. "I won't be able to call you Cinnamon anymore with all that salt seasoning."

A weak smile lit her face for a second before it was overtaken with extreme pain. "F-fucking b-burns."

"Wait until recovery. This'll seem like a day at the beach."

"M-my only day at the beach was when C-Cian pulled me from the lake. It sssucked." She was feebly pulling out another packet.

He chuckled before falling quiet. "It's going to be excruciating when I dig the bullets out."

"D-do it."

He pulled out a switchblade and flicked it open. The smaller size compared to his tactical knife would be better for digging.

Her bloodied, salt-crusted hand landed on his arm. "Sh-Shilo?"

"Here." His auntie limped around the forklift and gingerly lowered herself. "I see I slept through all the action." She grimaced. "Thomas was never stable, but I never thought he was more than hot air."

Her keen gaze went from him to Kaitlyn and back. She kneeled and grasped Kaitlyn's hand before solemnly nodding to him.

Having Shilo recovered and here with her knowledge—not that there was much more she could do other than offer moral support—boosted his optimism.

He cut Kaitlyn's shirt open and palpated around the wound. After discerning the angle it entered, he rested the blade on her bruised flesh. She hissed in a breath.

"Cut quick and deep." Shilo secured Kaitlyn's other hand. Strands of copper hair stuck to his mate's face, the color startling against her pale skin.

Chayton swallowed, and sliced.

A scream ripped from Kaitlyn. She arched and stopped, tried to arch again. Her body instinctively wanted to get away from the pain, but it hurt too bad to try.

He blocked her out, had to. Shilo was there to help her, he needed to find the bullet. Zeroing all of his senses to the opening in Kaitlyn, he searching for the bullet. Centimeter by centimeter he searched in a game of hot and cold. At some point, Kaitlyn quit moving as she blacked out, but her heart still beat—weakly.

Finally, he got a bead on the hunk of metal. He cursed not having dainty fingers to rifle through her organs. It was lodged under her spleen. One inch higher and she'd have bled out long ago, letting the silver take over. Pulling out another blade, he used the two like tongs to gain purchase on the slimy metal and extract it.

He tossed it behind him and cut up his shirt to use as a band to hold her flesh together.

Shilo released Kaitlyn's hands and waved him off. "Check her thigh. I'll wrap her incision and check for any other wounds."

No one argued with Auntie. He did as she asked and probed the area. "Thank the Sweet Mother, it went through."

"Does she have any more salt? I can see the front of her thigh has salt scattered all over, but the exit point will need a dose." She met his gaze. "The whole wound will, all the way through. As much blood as she lost, I'm sure the salt didn't go deep enough."

He sat back on his haunches and rubbed his forehead with the back of his bloodied hand. What he wouldn't trade for some water. The solution would be easier to spread than granules. Would the pain he inflicted on Kaitlyn never end?

One packet remained in her pouch. He dug it out and squished the contents into the gaping hole he found on the back of her thigh. Kaitlyn didn't twitch. It concerned him as much as relieved him because the next step would be as bad as thumbing through her insides.

He dug into his own tactical belt. While he didn't carry as much as his partner, he had more than enough. The incident with Tika had made him stock up.

Shaking the salt to coat his index finger, his stomach revolted.

Gritting his teeth at the rending of flesh, he pressed his finger into her thigh muscle, following the path the bullet took. He did that on both sides until he was confident he'd covered every millimeter. When he was done, his shoulders sagged and he allowed himself to relax.

"She means much to you." Shilo's intelligent brown eyes held no contempt.

Their mission was finally over, but the weight of his vow still ruled his world. His mother wasn't around to talk about it with and he found himself spilling everything.

"After *Ina* died, Zitkana hounded me so relentlessly, I caved. It should've been a major issue, but I didn't dwell on it until…" He gestured to the redhead stretched on the ground.

Carefully, he slid one arm under Kaitlyn's shoulder and the other under her knees. He hefted her to his chest as he stood.

Shilo tipped her head to the other end of the lumberyard. "If you don't want to go through the store, you can get to the parking lot through there."

She steered him and he told her about the events of the last week. Her hand rested on his shoulder. With no young of her own, she'd always doted on him. He hadn't realized how much he'd missed it since his mom died.

"Chay," her tone was grave, "you made a vow, which is exactly what they wanted. Think about that."

He frowned and adjusted his precious cargo so Kaitlyn's head didn't loll back and sway with each step. "Yes, it is. I think the only reason Tika wants to mate is because she senses how vulnerable she is."

Shilo snorted. "She should. Tika's no leader. She reminds me more of those girls on the cable reality shows."

"Auntie?" *Eya*. Reality shows?

"Shush. It's entertaining."

They reached the SUV. He loaded Kaitlyn and himself in the back and tossed his keys to Shilo. "Head to my *ahte's*."

She hit the gas and they squealed out of the lot. "My point is…" Her mouth pressed in a flat line. Her braid was askew and her clothes rumpled, yet she appeared unruffled about what had happened the last hour. "Your mother's death never sat well with me. My instincts told me it wasn't her time."

He cradled Kaitlyn's head to his shoulder and reached behind the seat for a bottle of water. The girl needed to start getting nourishment or her body had nothing to recover with. "None of us felt right about her dying."

"Your father was deep in the forest on a run. They said she was going to surprise him with a French dessert. Come on, Chayton. When did she make fancy desserts?"

"She was always doing stuff around our home. Preserving our traditions, trying new things." It endeared him to his ina. She was fiercely proud of her heritage, but wasn't afraid to branch out.

"Yeah," she grumbled. "Just saying, not many shifters keep a tiny blowtorch on hand to make a treat."

He trickled water over Kaitlyn's mouth. Nothing. He adjusted to use a finger to pry the corner of her mouth open and dripped in a couple drops. All the way to his father's house, he repeated the process, pondering over what Shilo said.

Then she added another tidbit that made Chayton think long and hard. "I just wonder, how would things have been different if your human mother was shifter-born with a mental ability, like maybe yours?"

Chapter Eighteen

Kaitlyn wanted to put her hand to her head, but had no strength to lift it. For what seemed like days, she hadn't been able to move, like she was at the bottom of the lake and the water pressed her body against the lake bed. Her mind was sluggish, body opposed to movement.

Whenever she put up resistance, struggled to the surface, everything went black.

She was sick of that feeling. Blacking out seemed more like her ability than anything else.

This time, she refused to go under. Everything lightened around her. Her eyes were still closed, but it was daylight and it poured into wherever she lay.

Where was she? The scent was familiar… The room she'd stayed in at Des's house.

She concentrated. One eyelid opened, followed by the other, then rapid blinking. Bright. It was bright.

Someone got up and drew the shade down. She squinted at him, but she'd already registered it was Chayton.

His hair had grown longer. It might be a full quarter inch. He was wearing what she last remembered seeing him in, but it was clean, same with his gear. How long had it been?

His face was somber and haggard. "Your recovery isn't done yet. You're going to be fatigued and feel like a steamroller ran over you and then reversed."

The corner of her mouth twitched. How accurate.

"How long?" She mouthed the words, her vocals cords not ready to work.

"How long were you out, or how long before you recover?" He waved at her to try not to speak again. "I'll answer both. You've been resting for four days. You probably have four more before you're ready to go back home."

Are you staying here? There, that was easier. She didn't want to know the answer, but she had to ask.

"For a little longer." A sad smile crossed his face. "But not to be with Tika. I swore myself to her, but I didn't swear myself to a timeline of when I'd bond with her."

She swallowed. The emotional pain of going back without him again, or worse, going back and limiting it to a working relationship, outdid her physical anguish.

"I don't want to tell them until you're back to a hundred percent. Call me paranoid, but I don't think Mato and Zitkana will take it well when I cancel this spring's ceremony. I'm sure now that I've been parked by your bedside, and will be for a few more days, they'll figure out why."

What's going on with the colony leadership? I doubt the hardware store crew were the only ones who thought the town would be better off without them.

Chayton sat back and kicked his legs out, his hands folded over his belly. "There's not much we can do if someone challenges him outright. Elections have recently become an option, but Mato's opposition would have to organize a movement against him and get the majority behind them to hold a vote. Otherwise, it's business as usual. Mato's still the leader and it'll still pass to Tika when he's gone." He shrugged. "Maybe they'll hold out and challenge her."

She'd die.

He nodded. No remorse crossed his face, just grim acceptance. "If she plans to lead, then she needs to be worthy of the position. She should know by now that she has to train, she can't rely on me."

Wouldn't they expect you to save the day?

"Probably. Doesn't mean I'm going to. Her parents knew I was a Guardian when they talked me into it." He fell quiet, his brows drawn together as he stared at the floor.

She watched him, something she could do for hours. This was the first time she could actually be blatant about it. They each knew where the other stood, she could drink her fill, yet she felt he was worried about more than laying out his decision for Mato and Zitkana.

Talk to me.

His gaze sharpened and she sensed anger roiling inside of him. "I don't know anything, yet. But Auntie alluded to *Ina's* death. The fire never made sense to her. I mean, accidents happen even to us. She just feels the circumstances were absurd."

She thinks it was arson.

The muscles on each side of his jaw flexed. So, he'd started to think so, too.

How can we find out?

His gaze jerked up to her. "If there's a way, I'll find out. This won't be a situation for the Guardians to handle, but for me and *Ahte*."

Fair enough. Her eyelids drooped, exhaustion took over.

"Sleep, Cinnamon. I'll be here when you wake up."

***

His promise was accurate. She finally groaned herself out of bed three days later. Every time she'd opened her eyes, Chayton was sitting in the chair. He fed her bone marrow broth and they talked about his beadwork and leather-working until she succumbed to sleep. They'd repeat the routine, only their discussion topics would vary from her love of shopping to his antics as a young shifter child.

"Sleeping Beauty finally gets her ass up."
Chayton tossed towels onto the bed. A shower had
never sounded more divine. And the bathroom. Her
body had finally tapped out on the broth and sent
the extra to her bladder.

She flipped him the finger and shuffled to the
bathroom. Any toiletries she'd packed were lined up
on the small counter. Her bathroom break was as
good as a luxury spa.

The basics were done and she stood in the tub,
under the spray from the showerhead. Once she got
out, she'd have to go back to work. Chayton had
cleared it with the commander to stay as long as he
needed. She would head back. No snowstorm this
time. Most of the last stuff had melted, the land
waiting until full-blown winter settled in.

She straightened with the creaking of the door,
Chayton's aroused scent mingling with the steam.
"Umm, I'm not done yet."

Her heart slammed against her ribs. They
couldn't do anything. Not with the way things stood
between them.

The shower curtain pulled back. Obviously,
Chayton didn't think so. He was gloriously nude,
and erect.

He stepped in and suddenly the tub seemed too
small.

"We can't do this. Not when you're bound to
someone else." Her body screamed that yes, yes
they could, and should, do anything they wanted.

Only this would be no frantic coupling. They were both of sound mind and body, eyes wide open.

Could she be with him and not hate herself for succumbing?

He cupped her face, his expression solemn. "I swear you will be my only one. I will find a way to be with you."

His words sounded heavenly, but she was no naïve little girl. "I'm still the shifter who was raised human, who passes out after every shift."

"You're also the female who saved my ass and was at my side when we took out seven shifters. You're magnificent and I will be the proudest damn male to be your mate. I need eternity with you to make up for how I treated you."

Holy. Shit. Tears welled. His sincere words unraveled her. Hot water beat down on them, shielding them from the world in a curtain of condensation.

"I ask that, someday, you'll forgive me."

She sniffled and nodded. "I won't ask you to quit being an asshole because then you wouldn't be Chayton."

He grinned as he leaned in to rest his lips on hers. He gave her a small kiss before pulling back. "I understand if you want to keep your distance until my situation is straightened out, but I need this, Kaitlyn. I need to be in you, feel you, know you're alive and well. This last week has been hell."

Standing on her tiptoes, she wrapped her arms around his neck, her breasts pressed against his hot chest, her mouth smashed to his. He made a guttural moan as he turned them to push her against the wall.

She twined her legs around his waist. The position placed his erection at her center. No more preparation was needed. After his sweet words, she was ready.

He slid inside and broke their kiss to rest his forehead to hers as they rocked and enjoyed being together. His grip on her inner thighs probably left prints and she wished they wouldn't heal right away. It was the only way he could claim her for now.

Withdrawing and pumping back in, he spread her legs wider. Her breasts bounced with each thrust. She was helpless to move with him. Her body was for him to dominate. Something they both needed.

His dark, lust-filled gaze caressed her body. A flush crept from her chest to her neck. He followed it with his tongue, not losing rhythm.

Her orgasm was going to hit fast. It wasn't enough. "Do we have the place to ourselves?"

"Fuck, yes. I want to stretch you out on the bed and devour you."

Being back in the bed again only appealed to her if he was with her. Shudders started deep within her core. "Oh my god, Chay. You feel so good." She couldn't clamp her legs around him, still helpless to his strength.

He pistoned faster, his own orgasm waiting to hit when hers did. Arching her back, she dug her nails into his shoulders. From his growl, he loved it.

"Come for me." He dipped his mouth to her neck and sucked as she bucked into him.

"Yes!" she screamed.

He let himself go, his roar echoing off the walls of the bathroom.

They quieted, their bodies coming down from their high, but not all the way. He was still hard inside of her and her sex responded.

He reached over to flip off the water. Droplets fell from the sharp planes of his face. She licked them away one by one.

"Two can play at that game." He eased her away and helped her out of the tub. He climbed out and toweled them dry. She yelped when he jerked her back to him. One arm snaked around her waist, his other hand tunneling through her folds.

"I think I missed a spot with the towel." He whispered in her ear, "Only my tongue can reach it."

He carried her back to the bedroom and she decided the rest of the world could wait until they sated themselves with each other.

Chapter Nineteen

Chayton calmly gazed at the irate male looming over him. Des had offered to come with him, but Chayton wasn't an angry kid. He got himself into this, he'd deal with it.

But getting to the bottom of the fire that claimed *Ina's* life? Both he and Des were invested until the end. His *ahte* stood with him in spirit.

Kaitlyn was fully recovered. It'd been five days since she'd woken, and she was finally through the debilitating pain that lingered after silver poisoning. He'd asked her to stay behind, in case he had to do something un-Guardianlike.

"I mean exactly what I said, Mato. I'm not bonding Tika this spring. Zitkana coerced me into a blood oath, and you both used it as an excuse to not train her like she should have. I also don't think it'll be right to deprive her"—or myself—"of a mate when she finds him."

"Is it that redhead? I thought I smelled something between you two, but figured it was just passing lust."

"That part of my life is none of your business. We're here to talk about your daughter."

"She's the future of this colony. And if that part of your life affects your blood oath, then it damn well is my business."

"Even if we did mate, I wouldn't be here all the time. My duty as Guardian comes first."

Mato shoved one beefy finger in Chayton's face. "You *swore*."

Chayton sat back and crossed his arms, glaring at Mato. "It was assumed I'd move back here after we bonded. But if she's in charge, I don't need to." The fight would go nowhere. He needed to get to the point. "How convenient for you that I wasn't in my right mind, having lost *Ina* the way I did."

Mato drew back, his nostrils flaring, the predator gleam in his eyes. His voice dropped to a hiss. "What did you just accuse me of?"

"How quickly you put those two things together. I wonder if most people would've—if they weren't involved."

A shadow lingered outside of the door. Zitkana stood partially off to the side of the threshold, a hard expression on her face. Unrepentant.

With a sinking feeling, Chayton realized Shilo had a valid reason for being suspicious. These two weren't angry because Chayton was making false insinuations. Their rage was because he'd figured it out.

Chayton planted his hands on the tabletop and slowly rose. "What did you do? How did it go down, Mato?" Rage vibrated through his body. He'd rip out Mato's heart, but he had to hear a confession, otherwise he sacrificed his livelihood. "Did you use your ability? Convince her to use the flame on her dessert and turn it on herself?"

No denial. Mato's chest rose and fell like a bull's. No remorse emanated from Zitkana.

Chayton gazed between the two, then settled on Zitkana. "You both did it. I was hesitant, wouldn't commit—*for good reason*. So you abused your friendship with my ina, waited until *Ahte* went into the forest, and convinced her to make a stupid fucking dessert." He turned to Mato. "You convinced her to turn the flame on herself. The fire wiped out everything, your scent, the influence you used. *My mother*."

He bunched to jump Mato. Clothing rustled as Zitkana stripped, probably to change into her wolf. It'd be a more equal fight for her.

The front door ripped open, catching all of their attention. A hulking brown man-wolf stalked through, saliva dripping off his fangs.

It was the most ferocious Chayton had ever seen his father. Never had he been more proud to be directly descended from an ancient.

Zitkana, not yet shifted, retreated down a side hallway.

Ahte ignored her. *You took her from me!* He was intent on Mato, the only one of them with the power to convince someone to light themselves on fire.

Mato had no time to undress and shift. He pulled a buck knife from his belt. His father didn't slow. Chayton was sure silver had to be involved. Mato would never leave himself so vulnerable.

Even though Chayton was closer, Des beat him to Mato. The blade buried deep into Des's belly. He roared and used his massive paws, tipped with deadly claws, to grasp Mato's head.

Chayton…stepped back. In his personal and professional opinion, Des had every right to carry on until it ended with Mato's head leaving his shoulders or his heart getting ripped out.

Zitkana was on the run and Chayton couldn't let her get away, but he'd need to stay close. That wound of his father's could be the end of him.

The back door slammed open, then closed. He charged out of the office, calculating how long it would take to catch up with her. Strategized what path she'd take to the trees.

He'd almost cleared the hallway when a weight landed on his back and an arm snaked around his neck. The blast of a gun preceded agony flaring through his shoulder. Crouching and flipping, he pried the arm away from his neck. It gave easy and he pinned Tika. Her eyes were wide and her chest was heaving. He was almost impressed at her effort.

He rolled off, but grasped her wrist. With a yank, she flipped onto her belly. His arm that'd been shot wouldn't work to secure her other hand, but with his knees in her back, she wasn't going anywhere.

"No!" she cried. He followed her gaze in the same direction the thick scent of blood was coming from. It wasn't all from his dad.

With a blood curdling roar, *Ahte* drew his hand from Mato's chest, a bloody, dripping heart squished in his fist.

Tika's scream of anguish nearly had Chayton forgiving her for her attack. His shoulder throbbed from her gunshot, but it was an easy enough wound to heal. As close as she'd been, the bullet had torn up his shoulder joint but carried on right out the other side. His arm hung limply at his side.

Tika sobbed under him. "I heard what they did." She dissolved into more tears. "But I couldn't let you kill them. I had to try."

He cursed. She needed to be dealt with, *Ahte* needed help, and the whole time Zitkana was getting away.

Did she know Kaitlyn was still in town, at their cabin?

He'd hunt Zitkana; he'd find her.

Rising, he pulled Tika with. "Congrats. You're the new leader of Spirit Moon. I'm afraid you'll be challenged for your position soon enough." He tightened his grip on her upper arm. "But make no mistake. Your mother will pay for what she did."

Her voice dropped to ragged whisper. "I won't let you."

Her shoulders drooped and tears ran unencumbered down her cheeks. She knew the truth. Thomas wasn't around to challenge her, thank the Sweet Mother, but the shifters in the colony wouldn't allow her to lead. If she didn't step down willingly, she was a dead girl walking. Mato had turned too many against him. The personal loss he'd suffered wasn't enough to excuse the damage he'd done over the years.

"You're still bound to me, remember." She was barely audible, but he heard every dooming word.

He glanced to Mato's heartless body and wished it was Zitkana's. His oath was to her, not Mato. As long as her heart beat, he couldn't walk away. Was tricking his mother enough to condemn the female?

Not if *Ahte* got to her. Chayton released Tika and shoved her away.

"*Ahte*." As he ran for his dad, he pulled salt out of his utility belt. After this mission, he wasn't going around without at least ten packets. He tossed them to his father. "Keep an eye on the girl. I'm going after Zitkana."

***

Kaitlyn tapped her foot against the table leg. The waiting was killing her, but she'd decided to give Chayton and Des the honor of revenge. She'd be more surprised if Tika's parents were innocent. And shamefully enough to admit, dismayed because—then what?

She sensed movement outside the door. Glancing up, she smiled. Cian.

I sense your impatience. Want to run and tell me about it?

She set the book down she'd been trying to read for an hour, but was still on page one. Could she be fortunate enough to cultivate a relationship with him? He'd saved her once already and wasn't here because he had anything urgent. Just because he cared.

Sounds like a plan.

I'll get a head start; find me when you're ready.

She watched him through the glass door as he loped off without waiting for her. All she had to do was shut off the lights and undress.

She stepped outside and shifted. The clarity of her already heightened senses picked up a new scent.

Zitkana?

A pair of reflecting, predatory eyes glared at her from the trees.

You will pay for taking him away from my daughter.

Well, he did it. He reneged as much as he could on the blood oath. *Come and collect.*

Teeth bared, a growl rattled through the night. Instead of waiting for the charge, Kaitlyn sprinted for the female.

Zitkana spun in a spray of dirt and took off. Kaitlyn put everything into her speed, but the other female was a fast shifter. What was she up to?

The female hadn't tried to use any ability on her. If she had, Kaitlyn didn't know what it was.

Zitkana's path took her through town. They ran through yards, past houses. Kaitlyn struggled to overtake the female but couldn't close the gap.

Chayton? Cian? Kaitlyn tried not to broadcast her thoughts. She huffed as she jumped fences and scrambled over pavement. So glad the ice had melted.

A large brick school came into view. Zitkana sailed over the chain-link fence around the playground. Kaitlyn followed suit. Over the soccer field, through the baseball diamond, Zitkana's trajectory aimed right to a garish playset.

The gigantic playground equipment stood on metal posts, stairs, and platforms. Thick plastic comprised the tunnels and slides.

What was Zitkana's goal? If she was this fast, why not run in the woods? Was it because she sensed Cian?

Zitkana's deep brown wolf transitioned to two legs as she approached the equipment. She ran up the slide into the middle of the set that stood a story off the ground.

Kaitlyn jumped to the slide that descended from Zitkana's platform. Her claws scrabbled for purchase and she slid back down to land on the dirt.

Zitkana's laugh raised her hackles.

"He abandoned my daughter for you." Disdain filled Zitkana's gaze. "Look at you. A defective mutt."

Ouch.

Kaitlyn prowled around the equipment. There was a short flight of metal stairs. Patterned holes lined the bottom and sides. Would those trip her up? They wouldn't get her close to Zitkana. The landing of the stairs stopped at a multicolored plastic sway bridge. She experienced the same slipperiness as the slide.

Zitkana let out a black chuckle. "What's wrong, Guardian? Why not shift and come after me?"

Dread sank deep into her bones. That crafty bitch planned this, made her shift and led her to a place where she'd need to shift back to get to her.

She'd be ashamed at being played so well if she wasn't so angry. *Even on the eve of your death, you're still manipulating people.*

Rage boiled off Zitkana. "I had it all arranged. The two shifters with the strongest and purest blood in Spirit Moon unite. No one would ever attempt to kill my babies again."

Kaitlyn's adrenaline slowed. Zitkana's loss was tragic, one of the most horrible things a parent could experience. It didn't give her the right to abuse and take others' lives at will. Kaitlyn was sure the female had done it for decades, possibly longer. Chayton and Tika's mating probably wasn't the only union she'd manufactured.

The thoughts clicked together. *Are you even Mato's destined mate?*

A low grumble reverberated from Zitkana.

Kaitlyn cocked her head. *So if he ran across his mate, what would you have done?* She knew the answer, but the momentary panic in Zitkana's eyes confirmed it. *Is that why Spirit Moon is so isolated? All this talk of bloodlines and purity, but you didn't want Mato to cross paths with the female he's destined to be with.*

"He loves me. We loved our children."

It doesn't make right all the wrongs you've done. All the shifters you've killed or helped kill over the years. For those crimes, you will face punishment.

"Then shift and come get me," Zitkana purred.

Kaitlyn searched and sniffed for a way to get to the slide opening. She could try bounding up it. At the very least, she might fall down. It'd be up to Zitkana if she'd come after her. In the woods with Chayton, she'd gotten so close to shifting without passing out. It'd been the last attempt, after so many, but maybe that meant she could try it fresh.

She calculated her odds, had to make sure it wasn't pride fueling her shift.

Chayton? No answer. If Zitkana had run off, he must be out in the woods looking for her.

She inhaled, slowly exhaled. Zitkana's bright eyes watched in morbid fascination.

If she let Zitkana get away, how many others would be hurt on Zitkana's flight to freedom? Kaitlyn's instincts as a Guardian wouldn't let her circle Zitkana, giving her more opportunity to plan.

Her instincts as Guardian also wouldn't let her do something stupid like pass out and be vulnerable.

No, she wasn't foolish. She knew her past; she knew her birth father; she accepted it all. It was just like firing at a target. Deep breath in, shift at the end of the exhale. Using her martial arts training, she visualized a seamless shift from wolf to human.

She reached the end of her exhale. Zitkana stilled, sensing the impending shift.

Kaitlyn kept her eyes open, focusing on the female, her target. *Come on, Guardian strength, don't let me down.*

The sounds of the night muted in her ears, replaced by the whoosh of the ocean that was thousands of miles away.

Fur turned to skin. Not only was she trying to stay conscious, she strived to remain standing, to take down Zitkana as soon as she had feet.

The world spun, but Kaitlyn held on. The sound of skin skidding down plastic alerted her that she hadn't noticed Zitkana move.

Kaitlyn tried to step toward the landing of the slide, but she stumbled. Fog fought for her mind.

Will not pass out.

Zitkana drew her feet under her and jumped off.

She plowed into Kaitlyn. Air left her lungs as she hit the wood chips cushioning the play equipment. Zitkana was on top of her. Kaitlyn blinked to clear her vision, but only saw the fist as it was driven into her face.

Her teeth scraped the inside of her mouth. Zitkana pulled back and punched her again. Kaitlyn's nose broke, blood gushed down her cheeks.

She rolled to the side, but the woozy aftereffect of the shift dulled her movements. Zitkana slapped her head back in place for another punch.

Kaitlyn coughed and spit out blood, forcing herself to keep moving. If she stopped, blackness would claim her.

Zitkana swore. Pressure released from Kaitlyn's chest as the female jumped off. She tried to roll again, but Zitkana was at her head, a firm grip around her neck and jaw.

Was she going to break her neck? That'd trump a blackout any day.

Instead, wood chips grated into her back and shoulders. Zitkana dragged her off the playground to the concrete surrounding it.

Energy rushed back into Kaitlyn's muscles. The night grew startlingly clear, euphoria swept through her. She made it through a shift without losing consciousness!

Pressing her feet into the ground, she tensed to spring up and out of Zitkana's grip when the female slammed Kaitlyn's head into the pavement.

The pain robbed her of breath, her clarity was gone. Kaitlyn faltered, but anchored her feet to carry through the movement. She wrapped her hands around Zitkana's wrists, but the shifter lifted her head and rammed it again.

Kaitlyn groaned. Her body wanted to curl in on itself. Her skull had to be spider-webbed from the impact.

"I'm going to smash your head until your brain leaks out onto the pavement. Chayton won't be able to recognize you. I'll enjoy eating your heart."

Kaitlyn's head was lifted again, but before Zitkana could slam it again, Kaitlyn shifted in her wolf. Zitkana gasped and stumbled back. Kaitlyn bunched to lunge when she was pushed out of the way.

A flash of white fur and snarls mixed with Zitkana's screams.

A cloud of warm, pungent blood puffed into the air. Cian's broad humanoid back blocked Zitkana, who'd gone limp. He drew his arm back, a bloody heart squeezed in his fist.

Whoa. Kaitlyn pranced to the side. He'd taken Zitkana down in seconds. That was the most amazing move she'd ever seen. Des had told her he'd ripped out one of the shifter's hearts, but to actually see it was really possible...

He shoved Zitkana away. Her body fell with a muted thud.

It was over. Chayton was free.

Kaitlyn!

Chayton's cinnamon-colored wolf bounded toward her, snarling, Des on his heels. The beast behind her stopped them.

She turned back to tell her dad it was over. Cian came to stand above her, Zitkana's heart dripping in his fist. His chest heaved, his fangs were bared as he glared at Kaitlyn.

Alarm spread through her. He'd killed Zitkana—would he stop at her? Would he know to stop at her? Would he go after the males?

He loomed over her, his gaze narrowed on her. His lips curled back farther. She ordered her legs to move, but they only twitched. How her life had come full circle. Now her biological father stood over her debating whether or not to kill her.

What would he choose?

Chayton and Des parted to creep around Cian for an attack.

Stop, she ordered them both.

Amazingly, they did.

Cian's gaze slid to his hand and the bloody organ gripped in it. He sniffed at it, looked at Kaitlyn. A sinister smear curved his lips.

Her heart thudded. This wasn't how it was going to end. She wasn't eleven any more. Her shifter psyche wasn't stuck in her trauma. *Cian, my other father decided not to kill me, I hope you'll do the same.*

A rumble gurgled from the beast's mouth. If he had brows, they'd be drawn down. The heart fell from his hand as he fell to his knees.

I overcame a huge obstacle tonight…Dad…you can, too.

Death. Blood.

She didn't so much hear words but see flashes of images from his centuries of life. *You have me. Tawny. Please, don't.*

Had anyone ever tried to reason with him when he went crazy?

Doubt it. They likely never had the chance.

The look in his eyes returned to the lucid green she'd come to know. His features smoothed out and he turned to his human form, the first she'd seen it.

Platinum gleamed through hair the same shade as Tawny's. The concern in his expression, one she'd expect in a real father, was replaced with horror. "I almost killed you," he rasped.

"But you didn't," Des said, walking forward.

Cian studied the blood on his hands. "She deserved it. She was trying to kill my daughter."

Chayton sidled up beside her. "She wasn't going to win, but you saved us a headache."

His words didn't relax Cian. He stepped back. Took another step. His solemn gaze landed on her. "I need to run."

I understand.

He shifted and was gone. Ever intuitive, Des murmured a few words to Chayton, also shifted, and left.

Chayton smiled down at her. "I have a mess to clean up, Cinnamon. Want to shift and help me out?"

Once wasn't a fluke. She concentrated and flowed into her human form. Swaying slightly, she blinked away the fog.

Chayton stroked her cheek. "It'll get easier each time."

"I don't know. I like how it ended up last time."

Heat flared in his eyes. "As soon as you and I are alone together, you're *mine*."

***

Kaitlyn navigated the highways that were becoming way too familiar. She wasn't done with them yet. Her and Chayton would make regular trips back to visit their family.

Their family.

A smile tugged at Kaitlyn's lips, but with great effort she maintained a serious expression. "What's the word again? *Natasla*?"

"Ha ha. I'm not exactly a baldhead anymore." Chayton browsed through radio stations. She'd put him in charge of music while she drove.

They were driving back to West Creek. Things in Spirit Moon were nicely wrapped up. Trevon, the male who helped her rescue Chayton, was voted in. Tika was pawing all over Trevon by the time they left.

"What was the thing I ate in the forest, the *sikpela*?"

"Muskrat." He chuckled at her disgusted expression and returned his attention to the radio. "Finally."

Classic country crooned through the radio.

She tapped her fingers on the steering wheel.

"Cinnamon, if you have a question, spill it." He reclined against the door, watching her.

"I was in your cabin to gather your gear and I saw all your things."

He nodded. "Figured as much." His voice dropped low. "You're going to be in there a lot."

This smile she couldn't fight back. After they'd claimed each other, he promised to keep doing it until he claimed her *everywhere*.

"Your crafts were spectacular and…they're important to you." Her fingers continued tapping and she shifted in her seat. "Are they something you'd like to teach me?"

His brows shot up, but he answered without hesitation. "Of course. Anything you want. You might have to trade a pound of bacon for lessons, though."

She rolled her eyes. "I'll chop it into the quinoa. You sure you don't mind?"

"I don't mind and *Ina* won't need to come back and haunt me for not passing my knowledge on." He shot her a devilish grin. "Besides, I heard about your porcupine showdown and I want to see if you know your way around a quill."

"One, fuck you, those really hurt. And two"— her smile faded—"I don't really have any family traditions to pass down." She lifted a shoulder in a shrug she hoped was nonchalant. "I would be honored to learn yours."

"Ours. And you do have traditions. Human ones, and I want to learn them."

When he said something like that…it was more than she could handle. She spotted a dirt road that turned off the highway.

He peered out the window as she exited and drove a half mile before stopping. "What's going on—whoa." His pupils dilated and his lust rose to match her own.

"What was that you said about claiming me everywhere?"

Thank you for reading. I'd love to know what you thought. Please consider leaving a review at the retailor the book was purchased from.
Marie

For new release updates, chapter sneak peeks, and exclusive quarterly short stories, sign up for Marie's newsletter at www.mariejohnstonwriter.com and receive download links for the book that started it all, *Fever Claim*, and three short stories of characters from the series.

About the Author

Marie Johnston lives in the upper-Midwest with her husband, four kids, and an old cat. Deciding to trade in her lab coat for a laptop, she's writing down all the tales she's been making up in her head for years. An avid reader of paranormal romance, these are the stories hanging out and waiting to be told between the demands of work, home, and the endless chauffeuring that comes with children.

mariejohnstonwriter.com

Facebook: Marie Johnston Writer

Twitter @mjohnstonwriter

Also by Marie Johnston

The Sigma Menace:
Fever Claim (Book 1)
Primal Claim (Book 2)
True Claim (Book 3)
Reclaim (Book 3.5)
Lawful Claim (Book 4)
Pure Claim (Book 5)

New Vampire Disorder:
Demetrius (Book 1)
Rourke (Book 2)

Pale Moonlight:
Birthright (Book 1)
Ancient Ties (Book 2)

19196965R00151

Printed in Poland
by Amazon Fulfillment
Poland Sp. z o.o., Wrocław